DOCTOR BOSS WITH BENEFITS

JC HARROWAY

Recycling programs for this product may not exist in your area.

ISBN-13: 978-1-335-99372-4

Doctor Boss with Benefits

For questions and comments about the quality of this book, please contact us at CustomerService@Harlequin.com.

Harlequin Enterprises ULC
22 Adelaide St. West, 41st Floor
Toronto, Ontario M5H 4E3, Canada
www.Harlequin.com

HarperCollins Publishers
Macken House, 39/40 Mayor Street Upper,
Dublin 1, D01 C9W8, Ireland
www.HarperCollins.com

Printed in U.S.A.

1 2 3 4 5 6 7 8 9 10 HDC 28 27 26 25

“I couldn’t possibly...” Greer shook her head again, as if convincing herself, but she didn’t move, only stared at him. “I mean, I’m technically your boss.”

Seeing the excited flutter of her pulse in her neck, Nate leaned closer and lowered his voice to a playful whisper. “I won’t tell anyone if you don’t.”

She gaped, but not before he witnessed the definite flicker of interest in her eyes.

“Look, in all seriousness, Greer,” he said, pushing his case, “I’m man enough to handle our boss-subordinate power dynamic. I promise to voice my consent or lack of, so you don’t have to worry about taking advantage of me, if that’s what’s stopping you.” He playfully raised his eyebrows.

She was obviously intrigued. And flustered, maybe even a little turned on by the idea. Oh yes, she felt this too—the driving force of two people who just clicked, regardless of logic or convention.

Dear Reader,

I hope you enjoy Greer and Nate's wildly passionate love story. In writing this one, I loved exploring the relationship hurdle of their age gap—the societal judgments, the personal growth Greer must embrace, the forbidden elements of their relationship that made it even hotter once they'd surrendered. But at the heart of any romance is the rightness of two people for each other. Why they work as a couple. How their strengths complement the other person's. Every woman wants to be loved the way Nate loves Greer. I hope you feel the highs and lows of their journey to love right alongside them.

Love *JC* x

Lifelong romance addict **JC Harroway** took a break from her career as a junior doctor to raise a family and found her calling as a Harlequin author instead. She now lives in New Zealand and finds that writing feeds her very real obsession with happy endings and the endorphin rush they create. You can follow her at jcharroway.com and on Facebook, X and Instagram.

Books by JC Harroway

Harlequin Medical Romance

A Sydney Central Reunion

Phoebe's Baby Bombshell

Buenos Aires Docs

Secretly Dating the Baby Doc

Sexy Surgeons in the City

Manhattan Marriage Reunion

Jet Set Docs

One Night to Sydney Wedding

Royally Tempted

One Night to Royal Baby

Nurse's Secret Royal Fling
Forbidden Fiji Nights with Her Rival
The Midwife's Secret Fling
Mistletoe Baby Mix-Up
The Paramedic Roommate Pact

Visit the Author Profile page
at Harlequin.com for more titles.

To heroes everywhere,
for being brave enough to fight for love.

CHAPTER ONE

OVER THE SPAN of Dr Greer Thorn's twenty-year career in emergency medicine, the night shift had become her favourite. It enabled her to prioritise raising her daughter. And while tonight was clearly going to be a busy one, she shared the shift with one of the more competent and experienced registrars, Dr Nate Hunter.

Ten minutes earlier, a code blue alert signalled the arrival of the occupants of a car involved in a head-on motor vehicle collision. Both had been critically injured. Knowing Nate assessed the front-seat passenger nearby allowed Greer to focus solely on the driver, a man in his thirties named Dave.

'I need another dose of morphine,' Greer told the staff nurse. 'And anti-emetic, please.'

Dave groaned in pain. The monitors sounded their invasive alarms. Greer could hear the same hurried energy from the other side of the curtain where Nate treated Dave's girlfriend.

'Lie still, Dave,' Greer urged, quickly administering the pain medication via the cannula in his arm.

Her patient's injuries weren't life-threatening. A fractured right clavicle from the seat belt and a fractured right ankle from the brake pedal. That said, he would need admission to the orthopaedic ward. He would, most likely, need surgery. He might even end up under the care of Greer's orthopaedic surgeon ex-husband, who also worked at Kensington Hospital.

As the painkillers worked to ease Dave's discomfort, he quietened and stilled.

Greer poked her head through the curtains into the next resuscitation bay and asked Nate, 'How are we doing over there?'

'I have a fractured sternum and pneumothorax,' Nate replied, his voice calm but pressing.

They'd only worked together for a month but Greer trusted Nate's clinical skills. Greer might be his senior and technically his boss, but, at thirty-two, Nate wasn't far off becoming an emergency medicine consultant. It seemed his patient was clearly the more urgent of the two.

'Blood pressure is falling,' he added. 'It's beginning to tension. I could use your help with a chest drain.'

Leaving her lower-priority and stable patient in the care of Harry, one of the junior emergency doctors, and the nurses, Greer quickly washed her hands and then ducked into the adjacent bay to join Nate.

'What do you need me to do?' Greer asked, their eyes meeting for a second. With one quick glance at the patient's chest X-ray on the computer monitor Greer confirmed Nate's diagnosis. The woman's right lung had collapsed and was at risk of being compressed by the free air inside the chest cavity, which without an escape route would build in pressure and eventually cause a cardiac arrest. A tension pneumothorax, if left untreated, was life-threatening, as evidenced by the piercing alarms recording the woman's pulse, blood pressure and oxygen level.

'Can you draw up some local anaesthetic?' he asked, then, to the nurses, said, 'Where's that chest tube kit? I need it now.'

The atmosphere was tense, everyone rushing to assist, bodies dodging each other in the limited space. While Greer and Nate hurriedly pulled on sterile gloves, a nurse quickly opened the sterile kit, tipping a scalpel, plastic chest tube, clamps and syringes onto the wheeled tray. Nate had already tried to decompress the pneumothorax by inserting a large-bore needle between the ribs on the anterior chest wall, but the definitive treatment was a tube thoracostomy.

'Kathy, I need to put a drain between your ribs to help that collapsed lung expand, okay?'

Nate explained to the patient, his voice soothing despite the sense of urgency and time pressure.

The patient's monitor alarms sounded once more, telling them all what they already knew: her blood pressure was dangerously low and they needed to act fast.

Greer drew up the local anaesthetic into the syringe. Nate swabbed the skin with iodine. While he injected the local anaesthetic and then made a small incision between the ribs under the patient's arm, Greer peeled open the chest tube from its sterile wrapper and connected the tap that would allow the air compressing Kathy's lung to escape.

Working quickly but expertly, Nate guided the tube through the incision with practised ease, and as Greer released the clamp and the air in the chest could finally escape, relieving the pressure on the collapsed lung, Kathy gasped.

'Well done, Kathy,' Nate told the woman, glancing at the monitor where the blood pressure had now stabilised. 'That should help ease your breathing. I'm going to suture and tape the tube in place and then we'll repeat your chest X-ray, okay?'

The woman nodded gratefully. Greer too breathed a sigh of relief as her stare met Nate's once more. She gave him a nod she hoped conveyed praise for his competence and quick thinking. As ED doctors, they were used to operating under adrenaline-charged conditions, but they were still human. Sometimes, it was impossible to be unaware of the life-or-death stakes of their work.

With the immediate danger over, Greer and Nate finished up with their patient and headed to the computer terminals to write up their notes, review test results and organise referrals.

'Well, the night is off with a bang,' she said, seeing from Dave's notes that her patient had already been admitted to the orthopaedic ward. Well done, Harry.

'I like the adrenaline, don't you?' Nate asked, shooting her a confident smile she couldn't help but return.

She'd noticed that when it came to his work, he liked to be right but wasn't overly arrogant.

'Sometimes,' she said, his curious expression making her pulse accelerate. 'Although nights are generally a bit quieter than this.'

And while she loved her job, she also loved parenting Lily, a role she intended to fiercely cling to until her daughter left home for university after the summer.

'Thanks for your help with that chest drain,' he said. 'Sometimes you just need an extra pair of hands.' He glanced up from the computer screen, his dark brown eyes holding her gaze for a little too long, as they often did.

Maybe that was another confidence thing.

'That's my job,' she said. 'Not that you really needed me.'

Nate shot her a curious smile. 'I guess I do know my strengths. And weaknesses, for that matter.'

Greer looked away, both certain that his weaknesses were few and embarrassed that she often felt uncertain of her self-assured, handsome registrar. At six-foot-three with an athletic build, dark hair and eyes and a charming smile, he'd been an instant hit with most of the single nurses and with the patients alike. Charm and charisma most definitely featured on Nate's list of strengths.

But for Greer, older, supposedly wiser and sadly cynical since her divorce, her intense awareness of him complicated their every interaction and felt wrong. Dangerous. Forbidden. It made no sense, but, in his company, she simply couldn't fully relax. He had this way of looking at her that made her feel as if he knew what she was thinking. As if he knew she found him very attractive just like those single nurses his own age. Hopefully she was mistaken. Because lusting after a colleague eleven years her junior who was also under her supervision must be a sackable offence.

Greer sighed, focused on checking her patient's lab results. Maybe she'd been alone for too long… After all her ex had moved on. And on and on. She'd lost track of his girlfriends.

'And I appreciate your help all the same,' Nate

said, his voice tinged with amusement. 'Not every consultant is as…collaborative with juniors as you.'

Taken aback by his compliment, Greer looked up to find that his dark stare had turned inquisitive as he watched her in that undaunted way of his. As if he found *her* fascinating.

'Aren't they?' Greer concealed a small flustered shudder, easily dismissing the idea he was interested in her beyond their working relationship as she'd been doing for the past month. 'But I'd hardly call you a junior. You have your exams, right?' she asked about the professional post-grad qualification required to apply for a consultant post.

He might be younger than her, but, career-wise, he wasn't far off being her professional equal. Greer wasn't one to pull rank, not when a registrar like Nate could very soon become a consultant colleague.

'Yeah, of course,' he said, his fingers flying over the keyboard as he typed.

Greer glanced his way again, something about the set of his broad shoulders telling her his comfort level had slipped. 'So are you applying for any consultant posts? I hear St Mary's has a vacancy.'

Nate finished typing his sentence and turned to face her. 'Not right now. Maybe in six months' time.'

Greer frowned, surprised at his reluctance to apply for the top job. ‘Most registrars can't wait.'

‘I'm happy to do things my way. What's the rush?' he said with a careless shrug. ‘I'm enjoying gaining the extra experience. I like to be good at my job.' He smiled again, obviously confident in his decision as he was in everything.

Greer scoffed softly. ‘I don't think anyone could find you lacking there, Nate.'

Within two minutes of meeting Nate Hunter, Greer had known exactly what kind of doctor he was. Calm, self-assured and decisive, he had the precise personality required for a career in emergency medicine, which could be fast-paced, unpredictable and often high-stakes. If he was something of a perfectionist, that could only be a strength in their profession. But he tempered what might be perceived as arrogance with an appealing degree of humility and maturity. Combined with his natural charm, keen intelligence and tall good looks, he had an innate knack of putting patients at ease.

Greer glanced down at his feet, wondering if his popularity with patients was in part also influenced by his penchant for colourful food cartoon socks. Today's were lime green and decorated with watermelon slices.

‘You like these, huh?' he asked, lifting the leg of his scrubs slightly to show them off. ‘My nephew bought this pair.'

Greer glanced back at her computer screen, flustered that he'd caught her checking out his socks. 'Your burger socks are my favourite,' she said, with a straight face, ignoring his charming smile and the way his dark brown eyes sparkled when he was pleased with himself.

She shouldn't be noticing his wacky sock collection, his expressive brown eyes or the way his scrubs showed off his muscular build and tight backside. Just because she found him attractive there was no need to lose her very sensible and mature head. He didn't wear a wedding ring, but he must be taken. He probably had a sexy girlfriend of his own age. Or maybe he played the field, used dating apps for steamy hook-ups she was too terrified to even imagine. Whereas she was a single, forty-three-year-old divorcee with a demanding job with unsociable hours and a strong-willed teenaged daughter as her main priorities.

'Noted, boss,' he said with a playful mock salute, his grin widening as if she'd said something hilarious. 'I'll wear those next time we share a shift.'

Unsettled by the intimacy of his promise, Greer cleared her throat, which had tightened the minute she'd started thinking about her gorgeous colleague's sex life. 'Right, back to it,' she said as she stood and logged out of the computer, slipping on her usual professional demeanour, before he thought she was flirting and reported her to HR for harassment.

Just then, Sally, one of the young, pretty nurses, approached.

'Dr Hunter,' she addressed Nate, blushing slightly because she obviously fancied him too, 'we're expecting a patient with status epileptics in Resus any minute.'

'I'll see the patient,' Greer said to Sally and then, to Nate, 'You finish up what you're doing.' She tucked her chair under the desk as if to draw a line under their earlier playful conversation about socks and her ridiculous imaginings.

Of course Nate Hunter wasn't interested in her, not when he could have his pick of women his own age. Just because today was the four-year anniversary of her divorce, a day that marked the years of solitude—no dates, no sex, no romantic connection—was no reason to fixate on her incredibly hot registrar. Or to imagine that sometimes, when he looked at her in that inquisitive way, *he* might be flirting.

'You're sure?' he asked, a curious look in his intense eyes as he watched her gather her stethoscope and phone.

'Absolutely.' Greer nodded, grateful to have a legitimate reason to escape him and that tension that must be all in her head. 'You'll probably have chance to pay me back later.' She tried to smile in a friendly manner. 'It's obviously going to be one of those long and busy nights. Not that I'm complaining. I like it busy.'

Less time to imagine fictitious flirtations with a younger man. To dread the prospect of *empty nest syndrome* once Lily left home. To face her fear of dating, something that, unlike her ex-husband, she'd successfully avoided since their divorce.

'Maybe I can also make you a coffee later,' Nate called as she headed back to Resus to await her next patient.

Greer continued walking, offering him a casual thumbs-up over her shoulder, telling herself his looks and compliments and thoughtful gestures were simply friendly and respectful.

Because even if the flirtation was real and not imagined, it was also irrelevant. Greer was a mature professional woman with an almost eighteen-year-old daughter. Lily had been through enough heartache and change in recent years without Greer introducing new men into her life. Attractive, confident Nate Hunter was either already in a relationship or playing the field where there were, no doubt, many eager hopefuls. Whereas she had the emotional baggage from her own upbringing, an ex-husband who worked at the same hospital to provide the near-daily reminders of the guilt and regret she carried over her failed marriage. And more importantly, she was

Nate Hunter's boss, responsible for his ongoing medical education and professional supervision.

For all his sexy good looks, nothing could ever happen between them and that suited Greer just fine.

CHAPTER TWO

IF REQUIRED, NATE COULD compile a whole list of reasons why he was deeply attracted to his very sexy boss. Aside from her beauty—long, dark hair, big brown eyes, gorgeous curves and a stunning smile—she had an elegant way of carrying herself that appealed. Combine that with her intelligence and a dry sense of humour he'd barely glimpsed and, for him, Greer Thorn represented the epitome of seriously attractive femininity.

And sometimes, when she looked at him and then quickly looked away, often blushing slightly, he knew she fancied him too. Knew she felt the chemistry that was obvious during every non-urgent conversation they had. The chemistry that had been there from day one when he'd joined Kensington Hospital and they'd been introduced.

Of course, instinct told him she'd likely never do anything about it, but as the weeks passed, Nate found it harder and harder to ignore. These days, he went after what he wanted. Because he'd learned the painful way that life was often too short to harbour regrets.

Just before dawn, during a quiet moment in the department, Nate headed for the doctors' office to make Greer the promised coffee. He was pouring boiled water into two mugs when the door opened and she appeared, her stare appearing a little fatigued, but her hair neat as if she'd brushed it.

'Just the person I was about to come looking for,' he said, adding a splash of milk to her coffee, just as she took it. 'The coffee I owed you.'

'Oh, thanks.' Greer smiled tiredly, taking the drink and sinking into a comfy chair with a sigh. 'Are things still quiet out there?'

'Yeah,' he said, choosing the seat but one to her right. 'I'm awaiting blood results and X-rays on my last two cases. And there aren't too many obnoxious drunks in tonight, which makes a nice change.'

He flashed her a playful grin, grateful that Greer was the perfect consultant, exhibiting a balance of support and trust in his abilities. He hated the ones who constantly hovered, checking up on his every move as if he were a freshly minted medical student in a pristine white coat. He worked hard to prove himself good at this career. He needed to.

'There's always at least one,' she said with an answering smile.

Kensington Hospital wasn't far from Kensington High Street and its collection of bars, pubs and restaurants. On any given night there were usually a handful of people who'd overindulged, lost their balance and fallen, wandering into the ED with cuts and sprains, impaired judgement and righteous belligerence.

'I prefer my night shifts a little busier than this though,' Greer said with a sigh as she sipped her coffee. 'Boredom is a killer. Too much time to think…'

Nate nodded in agreement. 'Keeping busy is an excellent coping mechanism,' he said, wondering from what unwanted ruminations Greer suffered.

Fortunately Nate's shift work, his free time spent with his nephew, kept him pretty exhausted. Because in those quiet moments… That was when the regrets came. The memories, good and bad. The grief.

'Feel free to get your head down for a couple of hours,' he offered Greer, because there were on-call rooms with beds for the extremely rare possibility of time to rest. 'I'll call if I need you.'

Some consultants made themselves scarce unless there was a serious case. But not Greer. She mucked in with the junior doctors, took her share of cases and not just the easy ones. She also took every opportunity to supervise procedures and educate those in training. Maybe that was another reason he found her so…intriguing. She was a definite team player and while Nate needed to be good at his job, he also appreciated Greer's support and years of experience.

'Thanks, but I'd rather push on through,' she said. 'I've spent years retraining my circadian rhythms for night shifts. Can't mess with the sleep patterns now.'

'Fair enough,' he said, curious about her personal life, of which he only knew the talk he'd overheard—that she was divorced and had a teenaged daughter. 'Is that why you stick to night shifts?'

Where Greer was concerned, he'd paid attention. While Nate, like the other registrars, worked a rotating shift pattern, Greer worked only nights. And he looked forward to those nights when they worked together.

'I've grown to enjoy them over the years.' She nodded, looking at him with answering curiosity. 'Especially now that my daughter is older. They weren't quite so easy when she was young.'

'How old is she?' he asked, certain that Greer would tell him if she wanted him to mind his own business. She could be firm but fair. Always clear and direct.

'She's almost eighteen,' she said on a mock sigh that made him laugh. 'She's in the middle of her A level exams. I'll just have time after our shift to rush home, make sure she's awake and wish her luck for today's.'

Nate winced, recalling years of exam stress. ‘What’s the subject?’

Fortunately exams were years away for Callum, although Nate’s sister-in-law, Maggie, was already dreading the teenage years without Dylan. Nate would continue to be there for his late brother’s son, but no amount of excelling at his job or helping out with childcare could atone for missing the signs that his brother was sick. Dylan should be the one spending weekends with his eight-year-old, hanging out, going to the park or playing computer games.

‘Further mathematics,’ Greer said, drawing Nate away from his guilt and shame and grief. ‘She wants to study astrophysics at uni next year.’

‘Wow,’ Nate said, impressed. ‘She sounds like a very smart cookie.’

Greer nodded, her stare filled with pride. ‘She studies hard, too. Do you have kids?’

Her voice rose in pitch as if he made her nervous. But her curiosity about his personal life gave Nate a rush of satisfaction. He might not be able to bide his time much longer before he asked her out. ‘I don’t. But I have a nephew I’m close to, Callum.’

‘How old is he?’ she asked, glancing at him with interest, as if she’d made assumptions about him and he’d surprised her.

‘He’s eight going on sixteen.’ He crossed one ankle over his other knee, flashing the watermelon-slice socks she'd noticed earlier. 'Thinks he should be allowed a phone like some of his friends.'

She laughed and Nate immediately knew he could get addicted to that rare sound. It drew his attention to her parted lips, to their curves and apparent softness, the pronounced cupid's bow he wanted to trace with the tip of his tongue.

'So what are you trying to avoid thinking about?' he asked to distract himself from the dangerously strong impulses. His attraction to Greer had been instantaneous. Violent even, only strengthening when he'd found out from the nurses that she'd been divorced from the tall, commanding Mark Thorn, an orthopaedic surgeon at the hospital, for four years. Rumour was she hadn't dated since.

'Oh, just life,' she said with a casual shrug. But her smile dimmed. She obviously hadn't survived the divorce unscathed.

'How it sometimes fails to pan out the way we expect?' he gently suggested, able to relate.

Being an identical twin meant he'd grown up never knowing life without his brother. Until the worst had happened and Dylan had died, snatched away at the age of thirty after a brief illness Nate hadn't spotted soon enough. Not a day passed when he didn't regret that he'd been too distracted by work and professional exams to see the signs. When he didn't berate himself both for letting Dylan down and for Nate's grief-stricken error of judgement months after the funeral.

She looked up, surprised. 'Yes.'

Nate shrugged. 'We all have sorrows and regrets,' he said quietly, his own mistakes a bitterness on his tongue. The memory of the night he'd slept with Maggie while they'd both been grieving for Dylan, both comforting the other, both immediately certain after it was over that it had been a terrible mistake, still brought him shame. 'Or circumstances we find challenging.'

'Or circumstances we've partly created,' she added with a resigned twist to her mouth.

'That too.' He nodded, holding her stare. 'But for what it's worth, I admire you. You work hard. You're an inspirational consultant and I know you're well respected by everyone here. And it sounds as if you've done a great job of raising that incredibly smart daughter of yours.'

She stared, blinking, as if shocked to hear such praise. 'I don't know about that…' She glanced at her lap. 'Divorce messes kids up. Today is my divorce anniversary, actually. Four years,' she scoffed bitterly and raised her coffee mug as if in a toast.

Nate touched his mug to hers, holding her stare as they both sipped. 'I'm sorry about the divorce.'

'Oh, don't be sorry,' she said, shaking her head as if flustered. 'My regrets are more to do with how long I allowed the marriage to limp along rather than its inevitable demise.'

'So you ended it?' he asked, understanding her regrets more clearly now. She obviously put her daughter's needs first, probably why she was still single. Whereas if the rumours were to be believed, Mr Thorn had dated extensively since their divorce.

But there was no way Nate could be similarly open with Greer. His ex, Mia, the last woman he had told about his mistake with Maggie, had been horrified. Unable to tolerate his ongoing close relationship with his brother's widow, she'd broken things off with Nate, compounding the paralysing guilt and failure he'd already felt by betraying Dylan.

'The decision to split was mutual,' she said carefully. 'We're trying to stay on good terms for Lily's sake. My parents are divorced, so I know the impact it can have on family. I never want my daughter to feel trapped in the middle.'

Nate nodded, his attraction now a persistent buzz, demanding more and more attention. 'Well, cheers to that.' Nate touched his coffee mug to hers once more. 'To fresh starts.'

She watched him curiously. His pulse surged with excitement. Now seemed the perfect moment to ask her out. He went after what he wanted and despite Greer's attempt at humour, to downplay the impact of her marital breakdown, this was the closest they'd come to a personal conversation.

'I don't know if you're seeing anyone at the moment,' he said, 'but would you like to grab dinner some time?'

Her cheeks immediately flushed, and he hid a smile of satisfaction. 'With you?' she croaked, her composure slipping slightly. Obviously he'd surprised her again.

Nate smiled and shrugged. 'Yeah, of course with me. Who else? I'm not asking for a friend.'

'I… I…' she stuttered, as if dumbfounded by his interest in her.

'I'm assuming we're both single,' he continued. 'We have heaps in common. Why not get to know each other better?'

'Because…' Her stare held his but she swallowed hard as if preparing an answer. 'I'm not sure it's a good idea.'

'Why?' Nate turned and leaned a little closer, witnessing the telling dilation of her pupils. Part of her liked the idea. 'Because we work together?'

'Yes, that,' she said, her breathing speeding up as her stare flitted over his face, to his mouth and back. 'And I don't really do dating. That is, I haven't bothered since my divorce.'

'Well, you said it earlier: it's been four years. Perhaps it's time to start thinking about yourself.' Like her ex-husband.

She shook her head, looking away. 'I work full-time. And if I'm not working, I take care of my daughter. That's really all I have time for.'

'But Lily will be leaving home soon.' Surely she was running out of excuses and she hadn't explicitly said no. Otherwise he'd have immediately backed off.

'I couldn't possibly…' She shook her head again as if convincing herself, but she didn't move, only continued to stare. 'I mean, I'm technically your boss.'

Seeing the excited flutter of her pulse in her neck, Nate leaned closer and lowered his voice to a playful whisper. 'I won't tell anyone if you don't.'

She gaped, but not before he witnessed the definite flicker of interest in her eyes.

'Look, in all seriousness, Greer,' he said, pushing his case, 'I'm man enough to handle our boss-subordinate power dynamic. I promise to voice my consent or lack of, so you don't have to worry about taking advantage of me, if that's what's stopping you.' He playfully raised his eyebrows.

She was obviously intrigued. And flustered, maybe even a little turned on by the idea. Oh yes, she felt this too—the driving forces of two people who just clicked, regardless of logic or convention.

'I'm certain HR would have something to say about it,' she said, her voice croaking as if her throat was tight.

'Are you?' His pulse surged at her expression of wavering hesitation. 'There's no explicit rule that I'm aware of against hospital colleagues dating.'

She opened her mouth to argue and closed it again.

'I've seen the way you look at me, Greer. I know that, like me, you've felt this connection between us. It's been there from the start. Since my first day.'

He'd obviously been right about their chemistry; she did fancy him back. She simply wasn't used to putting her needs first or she was hung up on their age gap or scared it might break a hospital management rule.

She sucked in a tiny, telling gasp of shock. 'But I'm older than you. A *lot* older.' Her breathing sped up, her breasts rising and falling as if daring him to lower his stare.

'That doesn't bother me.' Nate leaned closer, his arm on the chair's armrest only a hair's breadth from hers. 'We have insane chemistry. We've ignored it for a month, and we can continue to do so, but, until we stop working together, it isn't going to go away.' And they were still negotiating. She hadn't dismissed him outright and walked away. 'You're a beautiful woman. I like you. Respect you. It's just a date. We could have a good time.'

'A good time?' she all but whispered as if the

concept was foreign or her mind was going to some X-rated places.

Hell, yeah… Fighting his own heated imaginings, Nate nodded, the soft pants of her breaths drawing his attention once more to her entirely kissable parted lips. It had been a while since he'd dated. Maybe too long, because, as inappropriate as it was while at work, he really wanted to kiss Greer. To see if she'd moan his name, run demanding fingers through his hair, press her gorgeous body to his as they tried to get closer.

She sighed. 'I—'

But before she could finish what might have been another feeble argument and before he'd need a cold shower to calm down, the department's code blue alarm sounded.

Without hesitation, both he and Greer abandoned their coffees and took off running for the resuscitation bay, led by the flashing lights and deafening alarm.

'Seventy-nine-year-old brought in by a friend with chest pain, collapsed on arrival,' the nurse told them as everyone present acted swiftly to follow the cardiac arrest protocol.

'He's in VF,' Nate said, after glancing at the cardiac monitor.

'You defibrillate,' she told Nate as she relieved the nurse who'd been doing the chest compressions, taking over while calling for intravenous adrenaline.

With another nurse inflating the patient's lungs, Nate fired up the defibrillator. 'Do we have venous access?' he asked Harry, who'd initially seen the patient.

'Yes,' someone said as the anaesthetist arrived and quickly intubated the man and took over inflating the lungs.

'Shocking,' Nate said. 'All clear.'

Greer stopped the chest compressions and stepped back. Nate placed the defibrillator paddles on his chest to deliver a shock.

'Still in VF,' Greer said, recommencing the CPR.

'That's three minutes,' Nate informed the team, tracking the time elapsed. 'Administering adrenaline.' He flushed the drug through the patient's intravenous cannula and recharged the defibrillator to repeat the cycle.

At the next pause, the next shock to the heart returned it to a normal rhythm.

'I have a pulse,' Greer said, her relieved stare meeting his as if she was seeking confirmation.

'Sinus rhythm,' he said calmly, a surge of euphoria holding his stare to Greer's. 'Let's take bloods,' Nate instructed Harry, the patient more pressing than his connection with his boss. 'A chest X-ray and an ECG.'

'I'll call the medical registrar,' Greer told Nate, 'if you take a history from the friend who brought him in.'

Nate nodded, his head firmly back in work mode following their moment of honesty in the staffroom. Their conversation would need to be postponed but not indefinitely. Nate refused to see Greer's objections as obstacles. If she'd wanted to say no, she'd have done so. Obviously she, too, felt this thing between them, which wouldn't be silenced for much longer. And Nate had enough regrets without adding a missed chance to explore something with a woman like Greer. But for now, until he could once more get her alone and press her for a real answer, he'd need patience.

CHAPTER THREE

THE FOLLOWING AFTERNOON, after wishing Lily luck for her maths exam and then heading to bed for a few hours' sleep, Greer awoke still confused by Nate's shocking invitation.

There had been no time after the cardiac arrest to discuss it further. Greer had spent the remainder of her night shift busily admitting a steady stream of patients: one with an acute asthma attack, an unstable diabetic in ketoacidosis and two elderly women with falls who'd both sustained a fractured neck of femur requiring orthopaedic referrals to her ex-husband's registrar. And Nate had been similarly occupied with his own cases.

But now, as she stepped under the shower to fully wake herself, their exhilarating conversation was all she could think about.

For the past four years she'd focused on raising Lily after the upset of the divorce and having to split their assets and move to a much smaller place. What with guiding her daughter through her teens while also working full-time, there had been little time to analyse her feelings of loss over the relationship, or the emotional, physical and financial upheaval of the split. She certainly hadn't been ready to face dating again or meeting men who might have their own emotional baggage. Because who didn't at her age?

But maybe four years without any romantic contact was a mistake because, despite her many objections, she found Nate's sexy proposal, his resolve that the age gap didn't bother him, more tempting than she should. It would be easy to reason that if it didn't bother him, why should it bother her? And he was right about their chemistry and how much they had in common. He'd even surprised her when he'd talked about his close relationship with his nephew.

But…

Lily was still her priority. Her daughter had dealt with enough change. Having to move homes, being shared between her parents, Mark introducing her to a new girlfriend every few months. Greer had no intention of competing with her ex on that score. But Nate had only suggested dinner. It needn't go any further than that and they could keep it a secret, especially at work.

Emerging from the shower still torn, Greer brewed tea, reaching for a second mug when she heard the front door open and knew it would be Lily.

'How was it?' she called from the kitchen, trepidation hollowing her stomach. Maths was Lily's strongest subject, but you could never tell which way an exam would go. And no matter how well prepared Lily was, Greer had still had to deal with the inevitable tears and bouts of doubt.

'Terrible...' Lily muttered, slinging her backpack onto the floor in the hallway.

'Really?' Greer asked, her heart thudding. She hated to see Lily dejected, especially when there was little she could do to fix things. 'Was it genuinely terrible,' she asked, keeping her voice calm, 'or just standard terrible because it was an exam?'

'I don't know.' Lily flopped onto the sofa dramatically and stared ahead at the blank TV screen, clearly exhausted. 'Probably the latter...'

Greer placed a mug of tea and a half-eaten packet of chocolate Hobnobs in front of her daughter and sat beside her on the sofa.

'Well done.' She tapped Lily's knee. 'You're almost halfway there. I'm sure you did better than you think. Best not to dwell on it now that it's over.'

Lily sighed just as her phone pinged with an incoming text. She pulled it from her pocket and scanned the screen, her thumbs flying as they typed a rapid reply.

'That was Dad asking how it went,' Lily said with another long-suffering sigh, sliding her phone onto the coffee table. 'It would be really good if you two could communicate, then I wouldn't need to repeat everything twice.'

Greer nodded and silently counted to five. 'We do communicate about you. All the time. But yes, I can imagine how tedious it must be to have to repeat yourself. I'm sorry.' She concealed a wince of guilt, certain that Lily was simply lashing out, a hypothesis that was confirmed when her daughter wordlessly turned to Greer and hugged her tightly.

Greer hugged her back, stroking her curly hair the way she'd done since Lily was a baby. 'Everything is going to be fine,' she said in her soothing motherly voice. 'You've worked so hard for so long. I promise you that it will all be over soon. That all your preparation will pay off. Then you'll have a wonderful summer holiday and university to look forward to.'

Lily nodded mutely, her arms squeezing Greer's waist a little tighter. Funny that, even now, she still occasionally needed a mum-hug.

'You just need to keep going a little longer,' Greer said, 'jump these last few hurdles and in September you'll be leaving home for new adventures in Manchester.'

Lily nodded again and then looked up, her wide blue eyes full of concern. 'And what about you?'

Greer frowned, taken aback. 'What do you mean? I'll be fine.'

'Will you?' Lily asked, her own frown deepening. 'Because I don't want to have to worry about you being here alone when I'm in Manchester.'

'Why would you worry about me?' Greer said. 'You absolutely mustn't. It's my job to worry about you, not the other way around.'

'Because—' Lily chewed her lip and glanced at her lap, telling Greer something else was bothering her. 'I… I didn't know if I should tell you this… If you'd even want to know… But… Dad is engaged to that physio he's been dating.' She looked up uncertainly. 'He told me when we went for brunch at the weekend.'

Greer swallowed, desperately trying to hide her annoyance from her face. Why couldn't Mark have saved his happy announcement until after Lily's A levels? It was so self-absorbed of him to put his own excitement above their daughter's peace of mind.

'You don't have to keep secrets from me, darling,' she said softly, hating that their divorce had inevitably put Lily in the middle, despite Greer's best attempts to keep things amicable. Because she knew exactly what that felt like from her own upbringing, from her own parents' long-winded marital troubles. Her father's cheating then swearing he would change. Her mother repeatedly forgiving him but never able to trust him again. The endless tension in the home that, at Lily's age, Greer had been desperate to escape.

But no matter how hard Greer tried not to succumb to one-upmanship with her ex, Mark was selfishly putting his needs first.

'I didn't want you to be upset that he's getting remarried,' Lily said, still staring at her lap.

'I'm not upset about that,' Greer insisted, trying to calm down. 'Dad and me have been over for a long time. We both walked away from the marriage, which was simply no longer working for either of us. If he's met someone else and is happy, then I'm happy for him, okay. Don't you give it, or me, another thought, especially not now that you have so much else going on.'

This was exactly what she'd spent the past four years protecting Lily from. The breakdown of her and Mark's marriage, their divorce, were nothing to do with their daughter. After several years of dysfunction and resentment, they'd both agreed that, on reflection, they probably shouldn't have rushed to get married when they'd fallen pregnant with Lily after only a year of dating. They'd tried their best to make a marriage work and had succeeded for a while. But eventually with Greer's hang-ups, her tainted expectations of marriage and men in general, and with Mark's propensity to shut down his emotions and withdraw when challenged, the unpredictable demands of their careers had led to too many arguments and they'd drifted apart, existing side by side rather than as a loving team.

'I can't stop thinking about you, Mum,' Lily

said quietly. 'It's been four years and you haven't been on a single date. Unlike Dad…'

Greer laughed off her daughter's accurate observation. 'I've been busy. Working, being a mum, spending time with my girl.' She brushed a stray curl from Lily's cheek. 'But you should be focused on your own life.' Not dealing with the dramas of her parents' love lives. Or sad lack of one in Greer's case.

Lily looked up, hesitation in her stare. 'Dad's been doing those things too, but he's managed to find time to date and move on and get engaged.'

Greer nodded, furious with Mark for his thoughtless timing. 'And just because I'm single right now doesn't mean you need to worry about me. I've had other priorities up to now, but that doesn't mean I'll be alone for ever. In fact, someone invited me out to dinner only yesterday.'

She wasn't sure she'd bother getting married again, but maybe she should be open to casually dating the right man.

Lily's eyes widened. 'They did?'

Greer nodded and gripped Lily's hands. 'Yes. And I promise that if I meet someone I'm really serious about, you will be the first to know, okay? But until then, your job is to pass your exams, enjoy your holiday in France, leave for uni and have a wonderful time making new friends and meeting new challenges. Not to worry about the love lives of your parents, who've already had their time as carefree youngsters.'

'Okay.' Lily nodded, appeased. She hugged Greer once more, her upset seemingly easily forgotten. 'Love you, Mum.'

'Love you too,' Greer replied, flashing a brave smile, relieved that Lily, despite her parents' divorce, was so resilient and determined. She was going to miss her daughter when she left home, but would also enjoy every bitter-sweet second of watching her spread her wings.

'So are you going out for dinner with this man?' Lily asked, looking mildly uncomfortable, despite her concerns and her attempts to encourage Greer to date.

Greer flushed, as taken aback by Lily's question as she had been by Nate's. 'I um… I'm not sure yet.'

Long term, Nate obviously couldn't be the right man for Greer to take seriously. But he was charming and attractive. He understood the demands of her shift work and seemed genuinely keen on a date. Maybe the universe was trying to tell her something. Maybe dinner with Nate would be a toe-dip into the daunting world of dating without having to take it too seriously or trawl through the icky profiles of a million strangers.

Lily sighed with relief. 'Well, I'm glad to hear you have offers. Go you, Mum.' She stood, scooped up her tea, the biscuits and her backpack. 'I'm going to hit the physics books.'

Greer nodded and watched her go, her stomach sinking as it once more hit home how much everything was about to change. Soon, the affordable little nest she'd feathered for her and Lily after the divorce would be empty. Greer's life had been all about work, her marriage and motherhood for so long, Lily's absence would leave a massive hole. But it also presented an opportunity. Maybe it was time for Greer to re-evaluate. To rediscover exactly who she was as a single woman with a grown-up daughter.

With the first flutters of possibility dancing in her stomach, she pulled up her shift roster on her phone, scanning the days ahead to find when Nate would be working another night shift. Friday, three days from then.

The hollow disappointment she felt spoke volumes. He'd been right about their chemistry. Right about the way she looked at him, because he returned those same lingering, confidence-boosting stares.

Maybe what she needed, rather than a new hobby—wine tasting, a book club or hiking—was to stop hiding behind her work and her mum duties and start meeting people the way her ex had done. And maybe Nate Hunter, a man she liked, respected and fancied rotten, was as good a place to start as any.

* * *

It was three days later before Nate and Greer's night shifts coincided again. Nate had just finished suturing a scalp laceration in a fifty-year-old man he'd discharged with painkillers and instructions to see his GP to have the stitches removed, when he saw Greer at a computer terminal in a deserted corner of the ED. His pulse accelerated excitedly. She'd been constantly on his mind since their last shift. More than once he'd kicked himself for not giving her his number that night before they'd got too busy again.

'How are the exams going?' he asked, pulling up a seat next to hers and logging into an adjacent computer terminal.

'As well as can be expected,' she said with a hesitant smile and excited eyes that told him she'd been thinking of him too. 'I'll be secretly relieved when they're all over.'

He smiled and raised his eyebrows. 'So will she, I imagine.'

Greer nodded. 'I'm getting tired of saying "keep going; it will be over soon",' she said, sounding a little breathless, 'so I'm sure she's tired of hearing such useless advice.'

'But you're making all the difference by simply being there for her.' Nate tilted his head, entranced by her eyes and their long lashes. 'I'm sure she appreciates that, even if she doesn't always tell you. Does she have any plans for the summer, after exams?'

Greer observed him thoughtfully. 'She's spending a fortnight in France with her father. Then she has a summer job lined up for when she returns.'

'Nice. Saving for uni?' Nate asked, wishing he could read Greer's mind. But maybe he could. She'd already outlined all of her misgivings about dating him when he'd asked her out.

'More like for all the cute outfits she can't live without.' Greer rolled her eyes indulgently so he understood she and Lily had a close relationship.

They smiled together and Nate glanced around to make sure they were alone. 'We didn't get to finish our conversation the other morning,' he said, noting the way her breathing sped up as he wheeled his chair a fraction closer.

'No.' She held her ground, her chin tilting up. 'But I'm not sure there's anything new to say.'

'You could answer my invitation to dinner,' Nate said, relieved when she glanced down at his mouth, then met his stare once more. 'I promise that, aside from my terrible taste in socks, I'm good company.'

She pressed her lips together as if holding in a smile, amusement lighting her eyes. 'I'm very pleased to see my favourites tonight.'

'I wore them just for you.' Nate winked then raised the leg of his scrubs and flashed his burger sock.

Greer shook her head, but her lovely lips twitched with amusement.

Nate smiled and waited, knowing she was too direct to leave him hanging again.

'Listen, Nate,' she said, scooting closer, her voice low, as if she didn't want to be overheard, 'I'm not really looking for anything serious right now. Once bitten, twice shy and all that. And I have…priorities. Responsibilities.'

'You said that the other day,' he pointed out, excitement a rush through his system. 'And casual works for me.'

She swallowed as if her throat was dry, but she held his eye contact. 'What do you imagine could happen between us?' A steely glint of sharp intelligence he found incredibly sexy shone in her stare. Greer would never tolerate any games.

Nate raised an eyebrow, a playful smile tugging at his mouth. 'I have a very good imagination, Greer. But zero expectations.' He sobered. 'I find you very attractive. I enjoy your company. Why don't we start with dinner and just take things from there?'

'I'm still not sure,' she said, looking away, her colour rising as if her mind might also be imagining what might come after dinner.

He should be so lucky…

'But you want to say yes,' Nate pointed out, smiling. 'You think I'm attractive too. It's okay to admit it.'

When she looked up, he winked again.

'That's irrelevant,' she said, pressing her lips together, her face barely managing to stay straight as she slowly shook her head in mock disappointment.

Triumph surged through him at her confirmation she was tempted to say yes.

'You were doing so well up until that point,' she said, tutting teasingly. 'I'd almost convinced myself you had none of the arrogance of so many of our counterparts.' She gathered up her stethoscope and one of the department's tablets they used for accessing patient records, preparing to leave. She pushed back her chair and stood and Nate rose too.

'So is that a yes? I'm willing to wait,' he said, reaching for the pen she'd left on the desk and holding it out to her. 'It's just dinner, Greer. No big deal. If my socks of the day offend you, we can call it quits and forget it ever happened. No harm done.'

She glanced down at the pen and slowly reached for it. As she took it from him, Nate released his grip, his hand deliberately grazing the back of hers.

Her eyes flew to his, her lips parting on a gasp. Nate froze, certain she'd felt it too. The magnetism? The heat? The sizzle of really strong chemistry?

'I'll think about it and let you know,' she said,

visibly swallowing and tucking the pen into her breast pocket. But her eyes were bright with excitement and her lips curved into a small, private smile that gave him another surge of hope she'd eventually capitulate.

Nate nodded and stepped back. 'Like I said, some things are worth waiting for.'

And he had no doubt that Greer Thorn was one of them.

CHAPTER FOUR

TWO HOURS LATER, Greer was about to head to the break room for a drink and mull over exactly how she would tell Nate she'd finally decided to say yes to dinner, when a blue-light emergency arrived. She rushed to the resus room, arriving before the patient to find Nate was already there.

'What's happening?' she asked him, the thrill of their secret adding to the surge of adrenaline a blue light always caused.

'A four-year-old with fever and possible seizures,' he told her, his expression tense with concern.

'He'll probably need a lumbar puncture,' she said, her mind racing. 'I usually perform one in cases like this, just to be on the safe side.'

Nate nodded, looking focused.

'Want me to stick around?' she asked, sharing his obvious clinical concern although he was capable of handling this case alone. A diagnosis of meningitis or encephalitis, both serious, life-threatening infections, would need to be excluded.

'Sure,' Nate said. 'If you're free, that would be great.'

They headed outside just as the ambulance backed into the unloading bay.

'This is Toby,' the paramedic said as she wheeled the boy from the rear of the ambulance. 'He's pyrexial, temperature thirty-nine-point-two, GCS thirteen out of fifteen. No seizures observed but mum and dad give a good history of a convulsion lasting two minutes, thirty minutes ago.'

Greer and Nate introduced themselves to the boy's parents and, with the help of a nurse, Nate manoeuvred the stretcher into the resuscitation room while Greer spoke to the boy's concerned parents to ascertain any relevant medical history, allergies or current medications.

'Toby,' Nate called the boy, who was drowsy but somewhat rousable, opening his eyes for a second or two before falling back to sleep even while Nate examined him.

'Seizures in young children with a high temperature are relatively common,' Greer explained to the parents. 'We call them febrile convulsions and they affect around one in twenty kids between the age of six months and six years.'

While Nate performed a neurological examination on Toby, Greer tried to reassure mum and dad. 'One short-lasting seizure in a child Toby's age, with his high temperature, doesn't mean there's anything more serious like epilepsy going on. But we do need to exclude some things. The most common cause of the fever is something like an ear infection or tonsillitis or a urinary tract infection,' Greer explained, questioning them further about any additional symptoms that might have accompanied the fever.

'There's no ear infection,' Nate added, having completed his exam. 'So we like to run some tests. Take a sample of blood and urine and also perform a lumbar puncture to exclude a serious infection like meningitis, although that's just a precaution as there are no other signs to suggest that diagnosis.'

'He's very drowsy at the moment,' Greer said, 'which is common after a febrile convulsion. So he might not even feel the tiny needle we use to take blood and give local anaesthetic for the lumbar puncture.'

'You're welcome to stay with Toby if you want,' Nate added, 'or you can go to Reception with the nurse and fill out the admission forms, by which time it will all be over.'

When the parents had reluctantly left, Greer and Nate washed up at the sinks.

'Aside from the temperature and tachycardia, examination is normal,' Nate told her, his mind clearly working through the possible causes of Toby's symptoms.

'I'll insert a butterfly and take some blood,' she said, pulling some latex gloves from a box beside the sink. 'You do the lumbar puncture.'

'Sure.' Nate nodded decisively.

After Greer had taken blood for testing, she and the nurse repositioned Toby on his side, tucking his knees under his chin to flex the lumbar spine and open up the space between the vertebrae.

Wearing sterile gloves, Nate located the spinous process of the fourth lumbar vertebrae, cleaned that area of skin, and injected local anaesthetic while Greer supervised. Using a spinal needle, he carefully accessed the spinal canal and extracted a small sample of cerebrospinal fluid for testing.

'CSF looks normal,' she said, glancing over his shoulder as he removed the needle and covered the puncture wound with a dressing.

'Yes.' Nate nodded, peeled off his gloves and rested his hand on the boy's sleeping head. 'Well done, young man.'

Greer's throat tightened. It was one thing to know Nate was an excellent doctor—competent and dedicated and a hit with patients—quite another to see his compassionate side so openly on view.

'I'll organise the blood tests if you speak to

the parents and call Paediatrics,' Greer said, silencing her pager, which displayed a summons to Minor Injuries.

'You're sure you're okay?' she asked Nate, who watched the nurse cover Toby with a blanket and wheel him, still sleeping, from Resus to an observation bay.

He met her stare, a slightly vulnerable look on his face. 'My nephew used to suffer from febrile convulsions at a similar age. They're pretty scary from a parent's perspective.'

Greer nodded in understanding, moved by his closeness to his nephew. She wanted to press him on the relationship. To probe the sadness in his eyes, which seemed greater than his comment would warrant. To reach out and touch him. But she could do none of those things here and now.

'I'll speak to Toby's parents,' he said finally, collecting his stethoscope from the desk and looping it around his neck.

'Okay. Talk later,' she replied, unaware that the rest of their shift would be so busy that she wouldn't cross paths with Nate for the rest of the night.

By the middle of the following week, after several night shifts with another of the emergency registrars, Greer seriously regretted her previous reluctance for Nate's dinner invitation. Checking the staff roster for his name with the giddiness of a schoolgirl, despite being a medical professional and a mature divorcee with a teenager, was something of which she wasn't proud. If only she could stop thinking about him—the hunger in his stare when he looked at her, his charmingly sexy smile, the exhilaration of finally saying yes to their date and starting her journey of empowerment and rediscovery as a single woman.

Sighing after a long busy night in the ED, Greer finished with her final patient, an elderly woman who'd suffered a stroke leading to a fall in which she'd fractured her hip. She washed her hands and stood at a computer terminal to write up her notes. If she sat down she might fall asleep, although her feet were throbbing hard enough to make that possibility highly unlikely.

Glancing up at the clock on the wall, she saw that her shift had officially ended forty minutes ago. Dreaming of a long hot bath and her cool, clean bed sheets, she logged off the computer and headed for the doctors' office to collect her bag.

She rounded a corner and froze in her tracks. Across the department stood Mark. And he wasn't alone. He stood close to a woman dressed in a navy physio's uniform, presumably the fiancée Lily had mentioned.

Mark smiled sexily down at her, resting one hand on her waist as he dipped his head to murmur something that made her laugh. Greer tried not to stare at the couple, but she couldn't seem to look away. Mark, who sported a new, shorter haircut, was clearly smitten with the younger woman, openly flirting in the middle of the ED, and all before eight o'clock in the morning.

His fiancée, who appeared to be in her late twenties with long brown hair and dark eyes, was very attractive. Clearly forty-five-year-old Mark felt deserving of a second chance at love, another shot at making it last for ever. And unlike Greer, he had no qualms about their age gap.

Squaring her shoulders and running a hand over her hair, which thankfully she'd brushed an hour ago while taking the opportunity between patients to freshen up and clean her teeth, Greer approached the love birds.

'Mark,' she said, dragging his attention from his companion. 'Are you here to review Mrs Philips? Fractured neck of femur? I spoke to your reg.'

Mark's name had been on the orthopaedic surgery roster for referrals today.

Mark straightened guiltily, the look he shot her petulant. 'Yes, I was passing on my way to clinic, so thought I'd take the case,' he said, slinging his hands in the pockets of his smart suit trousers, his white shirt taut across his lean torso. He'd lost some weight to go with his new haircut and looked good. Happy and healthy.

'Greer, this is Cara Atkins, my fiancée,' he

added with only the barest hint of smugness. 'Cara, this is Lily's mother, Greer Thorn.'

Greer stuck out her hand and smiled warmly at the woman, who, on closer inspection, was strikingly beautiful. But then who wasn't at her age?

'Good to meet you, Cara,' she said, 'and congratulations on your engagement. Lily told me last week. Have you set a date?'

Greer didn't want to end up bitter. She bore Mark no ill will. As far as she'd known, and despite her suspicious nature over the years, he hadn't cheated on her. As long as his new relationship didn't impact on their daughter in any negative way, she was happy for them both. And if Cara was to become Lily's stepmother, Greer wanted to get to know the woman better.

'We thought at the end of the summer,' Cara said, shyly. 'Before Lily leaves for Manchester. We've asked her to be bridesmaid.'

'I'm sure she's excited by that.' Greer smiled, unable to locate a single iota of envy. In fact she'd spent the last five years of their marriage surprised it had endured as long as it had, concluding that they'd each clung to the wreckage for their daughter's sake. 'I'm happy for you both.'

Cara, perhaps finally feeling awkward, muttered something about seeing a patient and departed.

'Mrs Philips is in bay nine,' Greer told Mark, preparing to leave, too.

She was bone-tired and emotionally wrung out. Not from jealousy or regret over losing Mark, but from the growing realisation that, with Lily leaving home soon, with Mark having moved on and about to be remarried, Greer had a duty to begin prioritising *her* needs. To re-assess her dreams and wants and hopes. To be a whole and stronger person. To thrive. After all, she'd ignored her personal life for too long. She too deserved to be happy one day. Deserved for now to have a good time, to flirt and laugh and bask in the feeling that someone found her attractive.

'Tell Lily I'll see her Saturday,' Mark said as she turned away.

When she looked back, the eager smile he'd worn for his fiancée had vanished.

Greer nodded. 'I will.' Then she paused as another thought occurred. 'Is it still just the two of you going to France?'

She didn't really want to know his business, but she wouldn't want Lily to be blindsided if she had to play gooseberry to the newly engaged couple on what was supposed to be a dad and daughter holiday planned long ago.

'Yes, of course.' His stare narrowed, his defences clearly building. 'Why do you always do that? Assume the worst of me? Assume I'll let our daughter down or that I don't care about her as much as you do?'

Greer scoffed, refusing to play this game with

him any longer. The one where he put his work, his priorities first and shut down emotionally when challenged. Where he accused Greer of being paranoid and unreasonable. Where he refused to see her point of view at all. She could admit that, because of her past, seeing the fall-out of her father's repeated cheating on her parents' marriage, she'd sometimes allowed her unfounded suspicions of Mark to cloud her judgement. But knowing what she'd grown up with, he never seemed to be able to bring himself to communicate openly or reassure Greer.

'You're newly engaged,' she said, calmly. 'It's a fair assumption that Cara might want to join you on holiday. Anyway, have a wonderful time in France and take care of our girl. I'm off home for some sleep.'

And with that, she walked away, not for the first time grateful that at least, alone as she was, she'd achieved an invaluable sense of peace and no longer had to participate in the emotional game-playing that had become her marriage by the end.

CHAPTER FIVE

NATE ARRIVED TEN minutes early for his day shift. He dropped his backpack in the doctors' office and had just clipped his name tag to his scrubs when the door flew open and Greer appeared, out of breath and clearly a little unsettled.

'Hi.' Nate smiled, his pulse accelerating as it always did when he saw her. 'This is unexpected. I thought you'd probably already gone home.' They hadn't worked together for days. Plenty of time for his need to see her to build into a frenzy.

'I'm heading off now,' she said, glancing down as she calmed her breathing. 'I got...held up with a patient.'

'Busy night?' Nate asked, wondering what might have upset her, because his day was already a little brighter from this chance meeting.

'Yes, very,' Greer said, staring at him as if she wanted to say more.

Nate waited, looping his stethoscope around his neck while she watched his every move.

'About dinner,' she blurted suddenly, her voice

high-pitched. 'If you can wait until next week when Lily is in France, I… It's a date.'

Nate's smile was automatic, excitement pounding through his blood as he stepped closer. 'I told you I'd wait, Greer. But what's brought on the change of heart? You seemed upset just now when you walked in.'

She shook her head, her stare determined. 'Not upset. Just…distracted. I ran into my ex-husband. Not an ideal end to a busy night. Unfortunately he still knows how to press my buttons.'

'I can imagine that must be awkward,' Nate said and inched closer, intrigued that she'd changed her mind about the date and not remotely jealous of the ex, for all the other man's charm and intelligence.

'More frustrating than anything else,' she admitted breathlessly, still standing with her back to the door. 'Although I think his new fiancée felt pretty awkward. She fled not long after he'd introduced us, poor thing. Taking on an older man with an ex-wife and a teenaged daughter is a lot.'

Nate inched closer still. Her stare darted from his to his mouth and back as if she expected him to kiss her. So he'd been on her mind too…

'Well, I'm glad you changed your mind about dinner,' he said, catching the light coconut scent of her shampoo.

Her breathing sped up, her breasts rising and falling under her scrub top as she looked up at him with fiery desire in her eyes. She wanted him, maybe as badly as he wanted her.

'Of course,' he continued, 'I'd have preferred that your acceptance was unrelated to seeing your ex and his new woman.'

'It *is* unrelated.' Greer stayed against the door, raising her chin to look up at him with resolve and challenge. 'I wouldn't have said yes if I didn't want to go out with you. It never works out when you do something because you think you should.'

'That's good to know.' Triumph surged through Nate, energising him way better than his morning coffee. 'Although you seemed pretty against the idea the other night.'

He dipped his gaze, lingering on her parted lips as he imagined their taste and softness. The moans and pants that might emerge if he were to kiss her right now, to press his body against hers and unleash the passionate woman he instinctively knew was underneath her layers.

'All those reasons I stated still stand, Nate.' Her dark eyes shone as she tilted her chin another defiant notch. 'I'm still older than you. I'm still your boss. But you're right about our attraction.'

'I know I am.' Nate smiled, his heart thudding as he stepped closer still so he heard her soft gasp, felt the heat from her body and the thrill of excitement her closeness caused. While he understood the long list of fears she'd articulated, he wanted her ready to admit the things he saw when she looked at him. He knew with all certainty that if they ever touched, ever kissed, they'd be utterly explosive together.

She was breathless now, some internal constraint—maybe her hang-ups about being older or the fact they were at work—keeping her static, when everything else in her seemed desperate to act, to break this unbearable tension, to buckle and kiss him.

'Shouldn't you be out there?' she whispered, her stare flicking to the clock behind him. But she didn't move from the door, which she knew was his only means to escape the room.

'I have three minutes before my shift begins,' he said, resting his hand above her shoulder, fingers curling around the edge of the ajar door as if he might open it. 'And I'm suddenly in no rush. I'd rather enjoy the way you're looking at me a little longer.'

He was so close now, the scent of her, warm and tempting, tickled his nose. She licked her lips and looked up at him with obvious, unfiltered desire. Finally the truth. Answering need, surprisingly insistent, thrummed through his system, tightening his muscles, heating his blood, sharpening his focus to just Greer.

'How am I looking at you?' she asked, her bold eyes locked to his, her professional mask on the floor so he glimpsed the passionate, sexual, undaunted woman for the first time.

'Like you want me. The same way I'm looking at you.' He held her stare and dipped his head, his lips mere centimetres from hers so he heard the sharp inhale of her breath and felt the crackle of electricity between his body and hers.

'Can you feel it?' he asked, her breath brushing his lips, her scent a warm perfumed cloud luring him towards temptation.

She nodded, transfixed. Beyond them, the noises of the department waking up grew: people coming and going, phones ringing, voices droning. They could be interrupted at any moment, but Nate couldn't bring himself to care. The sound of his blood rushing through his ears drowned out every noise, even his own internal voice of reason.

'Believe me, I want nothing more than for you to kiss me right now,' he said at last, staring into her eyes as his body strained to put them both out of their misery and close the gap.

'What makes you so sure that's my intention?' Despite her denial, she was panting now, her big eyes blinking up at him, hungry with need.

And it would be so satisfying to give them both what they so obviously craved. But when she finally surrendered her last remaining internal battle and kissed him, he wanted to be the only man on her mind.

'I think the time for pretending is over between us, Greer.' When she didn't argue, only glanced down at his lips, so close to hers, he added, 'But I'd rather you kiss me when it's only about us and not him. I said I'd wait for you, but I do have some ego. When you moan my name, I want you thinking only of me and the way *I* make you feel.'

'I—'

He pressed the tip of his index finger to her lips, cutting off further explanations or excuses. 'Tell me another time. I have to go. But our time will come.'

Using every scrap of his willpower, Nate dropped his hand to the door handle and stepped aside, his regret and responsibilities at odds. Looking as turned on as he felt, Greer moved into the room, freeing up the door. She gripped her arm across her chest.

'Sleep well,' he said with a regretful smile, aware of the tiredness around her eyes. 'I'll see you back here Sunday night.'

If she was surprised that he'd memorised their shift rosters, she didn't show it, only gave a shaky nod and a smile tinged with disappointment.

With one last look her way, he locked down the need that had been background noise since the day they first met, left the room and the physical temptation of Greer behind and began his work day, one hundred per cent certain she, and their unfinished business, would be constantly in his thoughts until their next night shift.

CHAPTER SIX

THAT SATURDAY GREER had a rare luxury—an entire day and night off. In preparation for her holiday, Lily was eager to do some last-minute shopping for outfits, so they set off for trendy boutiques lining Kensington High Street, the sun baking the crowded pavement under their feet.

Lily chose her favourite shop, leading Greer into the cool interior.

'I'm going to try these on,' Lily said after ten minutes of browsing, adding a couple of minuscule bikinis to the pile of promising garments draped over her arm. She passed her bag to Greer and wandered off to find the fitting rooms.

While Greer waited, she idly perused the racks near the door where the stream of cool air from the air-conditioning unit was strongest, raising delicious goose pimples over her bare arms and billowing the hem of her skirt around her calves. Not that she was seriously considering any of the garments for herself. This boutique was more appropriate for Lily's age group than her own. Greer kept in shape, but her minuscule-bikini days were sadly over thanks to her Caesarean section scar.

As she had since the morning she'd last seen Nate, the morning she'd almost kissed him in the doctors' office, Greer wondered for the thousandth time what she'd been thinking. In respect of both saying yes to a dinner date and the almost kiss. Aside from the risk she might face a slap on the wrist from hospital HR for dating a more junior doctor, or getting steamy with him on the premises, she hadn't been on a date with anyone other than Mark for over twenty years.

What if the rules of engagement had drastically changed? What if she messed up, acted too keen or not keen enough? And what on earth was she going to wear for a dinner date with a thirty-two-year-old that could, for all she knew, be anywhere from a burger restaurant to the Ritz Hotel? Certainly nothing to be found in this trendy shop.

Greer had just identified a cute strappy sundress that Lily might like, when someone called her name.

'Dr Thorn.'

Greer turned to see Nate standing there, his charming smile wide with delight, his stare showing only a fraction of the heat from their last encounter, most likely because there was a small boy at his side.

She smiled back, her pulse flying and her knees trembling with excitement and lust at the sight of

Nate in casual clothes rather than scrubs: worn jeans and a navy T-shirt, sunglasses perched on the top of his head.

'We were just passing and I spied you through the window,' he said in explanation, his gaze sliding the length of her body down to her toes and back. He licked his lips, a knowing look on his face.

There was now an understanding between them. An honesty she couldn't deny and no longer wanted to. Their chemistry was a massive elephant in the room. An elephant painting itself red, waving a flag and banging cymbals, clamouring to be seen and heard.

'Hi,' she said, instantly overheating at the memory of how easily he'd sensed she'd wanted to kiss him that morning. No doubt he also knew how turned on she'd been by his closeness and the intent look in his eyes and the thrilling things he'd said.

Because she didn't want him to know that he inspired a perpetual state of excitement, she dragged her stare from his and glanced down at the child.

'This is my nephew, Callum,' Nate said, smiling down at the boy and adding, 'Dr Thorn works at my hospital.'

'Nice to meet you,' Greer said to Callum, who looked uncannily like his uncle. Same hair colouring, same nose, same deep brown eyes.

'Hello,' Callum said politely, his face lighting up with surprised delight when Nate pulled his phone from his back pocket and handed it over.

'Just that one game you're allowed,' Nate said with sexy authority, 'and only for two minutes while Uncle Nate talks to Dr Thorn about work, okay?'

Uncle Nate... Even that was sexy.

Callum nodded eagerly. He took the phone as if he'd been handed a pile of gold treasure and sat on the floor just inside the door to enjoy his few minutes of screen time.

When they were alone, Nate stepped closer and dropped his voice. 'It's good to see you. You've been on my mind all week.' His stare shifted lazily over her body, warming the places it landed as if he'd touched her skin. She might have complained if she hadn't appreciated his moments earlier.

'Have I?' Greer asked, her mouth awash with saliva at how hot he was and how he stared so intently, as if he wanted to devour her. But she needed to play it cool. She didn't want him to think he could read her like a book.

'Mm hmm.' He smiled confidently. 'And you've been thinking about me.'

He stepped another inch closer so she felt the heat from his body and detected the subtle spice of his aftershave. His words from that last morning at work slithered through her mind like a falling silk scarf grazing sensitised skin.

I want nothing more than for you to kiss me right now. I'd rather you kiss me when it's only about us and not him. When you moan my name, I want you thinking only of me and the way I make you feel.

She'd been too turned on by his closeness in that moment to explain that her apparent change of heart over the date had been less about her ex and his fiancée and more of a reflection of how tempted she'd been to say yes from the start. She'd needed time to come to terms with the very inconvenient attraction. Time to rationalise her needs. Her internal battle between *want* and *should* still raged. And Lily would always be her priority.

Reminded that she had bigger concerns than what to wear on their date, this insanely fierce attraction for one, Greer felt her nerves multiply.

'About the other morning,' she said, clearing her tight throat, saying her piece before Lily returned and she missed her chance. 'I'm sorry if my accepting your invitation seemed reactive. It wasn't. I was tempted to say yes the first night you asked me.'

'That's good to know.' His gorgeous smile widened and he inched closer still, his stare nowhere near professional or friendly. 'I'm glad. And there's no need for an apology. Actually I'm the one who's sorry. I should have let you kiss me that morning after all. I deeply regret being so…principled.'

Bitterly recalling how much Mark had loved to hear *I'm sorry*, Greer squashed her excitement. 'Too late now,' she said smugly while she hid her smile. 'You missed your chance.' She tilted her head towards Callum.

Nate grinned, his stare alive with heat and challenge. 'I hope there'll be others.'

Greer concealed a shudder. How could he turn her on with just a look or the way he spoke her name? How was it possible that every time they interacted, her attraction grew and her resolve to play it cool disintegrated? Yes, she was rusty at flirtation, but she was a mature woman. Only he made her feel…light-headed.

'So if it wasn't your ex that made you change your mind,' he said, 'what was it? I don't usually have to beg women to go out with me.'

Greer pretended to consider his question. 'I'd like to have seen the begging, actually. It might have swayed me sooner.'

When he only smiled as if delighted by their banter she continued. 'Your invitation made me realise that, after four years, it might be time for a casual date. Turns out, you were right. This is about us.'

Nate's stare darkened. Then he cupped his hand around his ear and said, 'Sorry, could you repeat what came after “turns out”? I didn’t quite catch it.’ He smiled triumphantly.

Greer bit her lip to hold in the return smile that threatened. His gaze fell to her mouth as she sucked in a ragged breath that seemed too low in oxygen. Was he thinking about kissing her? Did he imagine she might kiss him here, in a busy shop with his nephew close by? She was so out of practice with this stuff, but now she couldn’t scrub the idea of kissing him from her mind.

‘I like the dress,’ he said, glancing down to where she still clutched the garment she’d picked out for Lily in her fist.

He looked at her as if he wanted to see Greer in the strappy creation. Or even out of it. And her knees quivered with lust. It had been so long…

Greer swallowed hard. How did he manage to make nearly every word that came out of his mouth when they were alone sound sexy? That was another concern—what if all this chemistry they shared led to kissing on their date and then to sex? It had been more than four years for Greer and even then, for the previous twenty years, with the same man.

‘It’s for my daughter,’ she said, refusing to be anything she wasn’t. ‘She’s in the changing rooms. I’m most comfortable in jeans.’

And she didn’t need to overthink the sex thing today. Even if she wanted to peel him out of those clothes, they each had plans.

'Where are you two off to?' She glanced over at Callum, who was still engrossed in the phone.

'We're going to the park and then the movies,' Nate said. 'On my Saturdays off I often hang out with Callum to give his mum a break.'

'That's...awesome,' she said, trying and failing to hide her surprise.

'Is it?' he asked, amused.

Greer flushed. 'I just assumed, after working a sixty-hour week, that your weekends would be filled with...social events.' She'd imagined wild parties and numerous dates and casual hook-ups, because Nate was in the prime of his life, hot and single. 'He looks like you,' she added to cover her body's overheated reaction to the idea of Nate's sex life.

Nate's confident smile faltered, a sadness shifting behind his eyes. 'His father and I were identical twins. My brother, Dylan, died two years ago. Hodgkin lymphoma.'

Greer gasped, her hand automatically reaching for his arm. 'Oh, Nate, I'm so sorry,' she whispered, her heart aching for little Callum and for Nate. When he'd mentioned giving Callum's mum a break, she'd assumed the woman was Nate's sister rather than sister-in-law. But this explained why he was so close to the boy.

He shrugged and Greer dropped her hand, the palm tingling from the illicit heat of his skin, the softness of his arm hair and the firmness of his defined forearm muscles.

'Thank you,' he murmured. 'So do you have any plans for when Lily is away?' he asked, changing the subject. 'Are you taking any time off? I hear we're in for a summer of heatwaves.'

'I haven't planned to go anywhere. I'm not sure I can face all the traffic. I might take a few days' leave and just stay home, read all the books I'm normally too busy for and enjoy London and having the flat to myself.'

He nodded and just then, as Nate continued to stare, his smiling eyes doing the talking, Greer became aware of another person joining them.

'Lily,' she said, stepping back from Nate as guiltily as if she'd been plastered all over him, which in her head she had. 'This is a work colleague of mine, Dr Hunter. Nate...' she bumbled, overtalking to cover her embarrassment. She'd completely forgotten about Lily.

How could she? And would her super-smart daughter notice that she and Nate were...friendly?

'The budding astrophysicist,' Nate said calmly, shaking Lily's hand. 'Your mum's been telling the emergency staff how hard you've worked for your A levels. I bet you're glad to have them behind you.'

'Hi,' Lily said, smiling distractedly. 'Yeah, I am. Now it's just a waiting game for the results. Oh, I like that dress. Is it for me?'

Greer nodded and Lily took the garment in exchange for the two tiny bikinis and an armful of tops and shorts that had clearly passed the try-on test.

'Do you mind waiting a while longer while I try it on?' Lily asked Greer, obviously unsuspecting of her and Nate, maybe because of his age.

But then why would Lily suspect anything? While it was socially acceptable for Mark to marry a twenty-something, society was unfairly less forgiving of an older woman, younger man dynamic. Not that Greer was eager to marry again, anyway.

'Of course,' Greer said. 'I'll wait here.'

Lily rushed off and when Greer once more caught Nate's eye, she sighed. 'I haven't told her about you,' she confessed with a wince. 'I've mentioned that someone has invited me out to dinner, just not who or that I've said yes.'

Nate shrugged. 'Hey, it's fine.' He flicked a glance towards Callum. 'We all have our secrets. I don't mind being yours. In fact—' he stepped closer once more '—it's flattering. Kind of sexy in a taboo kind of way.' He waggled his eyebrows suggestively.

Greer flushed and then frowned, curious as to what Nate's secret was and guilty that she'd made him hers. 'It's just that Lily has a lot going on at the moment, what with her father getting remarried. I want her to enjoy her holiday.'

Nate nodded in understanding.

'I...' she went on, 'well, I promised myself when I got divorced that I wouldn't play games of one-upmanship with my ex. I don't want Lily to ever feel like she's trapped in the middle. That her loyalties are torn between her father and me. I grew up like that with my parents and I don't want the same for her.'

'Of course not.' Nate frowned. 'I understand that she's your priority, Greer. We haven't even been out yet so there's nothing to tell anyway. And it's just our business, right?'

Relieved that he was so emotionally mature and articulate, Greer nodded. 'I meant to ask where you had planned for dinner, just so I know what to wear. Jeans or fancy.'

'What's your favourite type of restaurant?' he asked, his eyes smiling as if he couldn't wait.

'Oh, I like everything.' She waved her hand dismissively, flustered because her nerves were back. Would they have anything to talk about? Would she come across as desperate if she kissed him at the end of the night? Would it be awkward at work the next day?

'That's not an answer, Greer,' he said softly, his stare once more penetrating hers. 'Why don't you pick your favourite restaurant close to where you live? Because I'll eat anything, and I'm happy to travel from Shepherd's Bush.'

'My favourite is Greek,' she said. 'There's a

taverna called Diamanto's off the Cromwell Road that's really good. I took Lily there for her birthday last year.'

'Sounds perfect.'

As Callum ambled over and passed Nate the phone, his time clearly up, Greer stepped back, away from the delicious heat and scent of him and the bubble of intimacy they'd created among the racks of clothing.

'Thanks, mate,' Nate said, taking the phone from his nephew. But rather than return it to his pocket, he held it out to Greer, his stare full of secret, grown-up, unspoken communication. 'I only have your work number.'

Reading his meaning, Greer quickly typed her contact info into his phone, the illicit thrill of simply giving a man her private number after all this time making her belly tremble.

'Thanks,' Nate said, his voice low and husky. 'Now we can decide on a day that works.'

Greer nodded, certain her eagerness must be written all over her face. 'Bye, Callum,' she said. 'Enjoy the movies.'

After that sexually charged interaction, she needed a second in order to pull herself together before Lily came back.

'I'll see you tomorrow night for our shift,' Nate said, the parting look he shot her hot enough to melt the tarmac on the road outside.

Shaking inside, she watched him leave, his

hand on Callum's shoulder as they smiled at each other. By the time Lily returned from the changing rooms for the second time, Greer had almost brought her excited breathing under control enough to act normally. But when her phone pinged a moment later, his text, the two simple words, Nate's number, were enough to shunt her back into a state of frantic excitement. So much for playing it cool…

CHAPTER SEVEN

SUNDAY NIGHT THE emergency department was frantically busy. Nate and Greer had no opportunity to speak, as case after case rolled through the doors. But as frustrating as it was to have no time alone with Greer, Nate had the memory of their almost kiss and her messages to keep him warm.

She'd been the one to initiate contact after he'd sent that initial text, suggesting Thursday evening for their dinner date at Diamanto's. They'd even chatted about their Sundays, Greer's enjoying a quiet day at home alone and walking in the park and his playing social five-aside football in Shepherd's Bush before heading into work.

By 4:00 a.m., Nate was in the middle of treating his latest patient—a seventy-eight-year-old man with dizziness and fainting spells due to bradycardia or a slow heart rate—when the man went into cardiac arrest and the heart monitor sounded an ear-splitting alarm.

'Call the crash team,' Nate called, quickly

commencing chest compressions while a nurse inflated the man's lungs with a bag and mask.

Within seconds, Greer and a few others arrived, looking to Nate for a history.

'He came in with dizziness and was in complete heart block,' Nate told her, maintaining the rhythm. 'I set up transcutaneous pacing and was just about to insert a central line when he collapsed. Now in asystole.'

Greer nodded and, in keeping with the protocol, administered a dose of intravenous adrenaline. When they paused CPR to check for a pulse, Greer's stare met his.

'I've got one,' she said just as the anaesthetist arrived to monitor the patient's breathing.

'Let's get that central line in and a temporary pacemaker before he collapses again.' Nate moved to the head of the stretcher and quickly established venous access in the right side of the man's neck. Using ultrasound guidance, Nate then passed the cardiac pacing wire through the venous catheter in the internal jugular vein, advancing the tip of the wire until it was situated in the apex of the right ventricle, where it could stimulate the heart to beat at a more effective rate.

'That's a good position,' Greer said, watching his progress on the monitor.

Nate nodded, satisfied with the procedure. With the temporary transvenous pacemaker set to eighty beats per minute, Nate peeled off his sterile gloves, relieved to have successfully resuscitated and treated his patient in spite of the cardiac arrest.

'Call the radiologist back for a repeat chest X-ray,' he told Harry. 'I'll call Cardiology and make a referral.' The man would need a permanent pacemaker fitted under anaesthetic.

With the patient now stable, Nate called the cardiology registrar on call, looking around to find Greer at his elbow.

'Well done,' she said, her eyes saying more than her words. 'For keeping your cool in that situation.'

'Thanks for your help.' As usual, Nate appreciated her support.

'I'd better get back,' she said, regret in the minute tightening of her mouth. 'I was in the middle of admitting another patient.'

'Of course.' Nate nodded, his adrenaline following the emergency draining away so he wished they could snatch a moment to themselves.

'Maybe we'll get a chance for a break soon,' she said, her shift clearly as hectic as his.

'We can hope,' he said with a small smile, his mind on his patient and the test results.

Before she stepped away, Greer hesitated, her lips pressed together as if she wanted to say more but was holding back. Clearly they both were.

Looking forward to their date on Thursday, Nate watched Greer leave and then got back to work.

By 5:30 a.m., the rush of new patients had slowed to almost nothing. Needing to wake herself up after a long hectic night, Greer visited the bathroom, splashed cold water on her face, cleaned her teeth and brushed out the tangles in her hair, feeling instantly more awake. In the moment of quiet, she pulled out her phone and reread the messages she'd received from Nate earlier that day, scouring each promising word as she allowed her excitement for their date to finally spill free.

Hope Lily arrived safely in France.

Thursday night works for me.

Looking forward to my next night shift.

Dragging in a shaky breath that did nothing to settle the flutters in her chest, she pocketed the phone and was just heading for the doctors' office to make a reviving cup of coffee, when Nate came around the corner, obviously headed for the same destination.

'How's it going with you?' she asked, her voice catching on a breathless thrill and her fatigue from moments ago evaporating.

How could she be so pleased to see someone she saw all the time? How could a simple smile from him affect her so strongly? If she wasn't careful, a beady-eyed colleague would pick up on how much she fancied Nate. And what then? Would she be called to HR? Would word spread to Mark and then to Lily? She needed to be really careful.

'All good,' he said, following her into the room. 'My pacemaker patient is stable on Cardiac Intensive Care. Since then it's just been cuts and sprains.'

'That's good news,' she said, flicking on the kettle to cover her awareness that the last time they were alone, in the shop yesterday, there was some full-on, non-verbal, X-rated communication happening.

'I couldn't say it earlier,' he said, staring with sincerity, 'but I always appreciate your calm guidance. If no one has told you lately, you're a great emergency doctor and an astounding colleague. I'm lucky to work with you.'

'Thank you.' Greer warmed at his compliment, even as shame for her unprofessional thoughts heated her cheeks. Needing to say something else to break the unspoken tension, she glanced at his feet. 'It's been so busy tonight, I haven't even had a chance to check out today's socks.'

She was nervous again, deflecting, struggling

to be vulnerable with him because the last time she'd been that way with a man she'd been let down, hurt, the relationship abandoned.

But this flirtation with Nate was helping her to feel more resilient, hopeful for the future. Certain that as a single, soon-to-be-childless woman, she could one day have a relationship on her terms. With Lily gone to France, she'd had a taste of what her future would look like. The flat was too quiet, but Greer also had space to put her own needs first. To play *her* music and enjoy uninterrupted long soaks in the bath and to find her wardrobe unrifled.

'Hot dogs.' Nate grinned and raised the leg of his scrub trousers, showing the socks off.

'Stop,' she teased, her stomach rumbling. 'I could murder a hot dog right about now. Somehow an apple just won't be the same.' Because she knew he took his coffee the same as hers, she made two mugs and slid one over to him.

'Thanks,' he said, with the same secret smile he'd worn yesterday. 'But now that you've raised the idea, I'm starving for a hot dog, too. What have you done to me?'

She laughed. 'Maybe we should cancel Diamanto's,' she suggested playfully.

'No way. I'm looking forward to it.'

Greer's nervous smile faded when, instead of

taking his coffee and sitting down, he stepped closer so her pulse leapt wildly.

'I'd like to pick you up for our date, if that's okay,' he said, his voice low and intimate-sounding.

How...gallant.

'But I'm happy to meet you at the restaurant if you prefer,' he finished, that intense look back on his face.

Greer shuddered and hesitated, her heart banging against her ribs. 'You can pick me up if you want. I live in South Kensington, flat two, Willow Gardens.'

'Great.' He glanced down at her mouth. 'I'll be there. Seven fifteen.'

Greer inhaled a slow shaky breath and nodded, desperately trying to keep her eyes on his and not slide them to his lips and lower, to that triangle of manly chest exposed by the V of his scrub top, and on to his broad shoulders and well-defined pecs… How would it feel to be held in those strong arms? To be desired again? To burn with first-time lust?

'I'm warning you now,' she said, her voice catching, 'I haven't been on a first date for a long time.' While she was excited to dress up and confident that she could maintain suitable over-dinner conversation, her biggest concern was whether she should kiss him at the end of the date.

'I'm not worried about that,' he said, unmoving but for the rapid surging of his carotid pulse. 'Are you nervous?'

'A bit,' she admitted, blinking up at him. 'But I'm looking forward to it, too.' She wanted the time between now and Thursday to fly. She wanted to enjoy this undeniable chemistry between them away from prying eyes. To forget she needed to keep them a secret, from work, from Lily, even from Mark, who would no doubt have something dismissive to say if he found out.

'I'm pretty sure that when it comes to dating nothing's changed,' he said with a playful smile. 'We eat, we talk, I ask if I can see you again.'

Greer fought a smile. 'How do you know you'll want to see me again?'

He tilted his head, a *don't be stupid* expression on his face. 'I'm already looking forward to our second date.'

Greer inhaled. He looked at her with hunger and heat. His height made her feel feminine. His hypnotic hold over her felt dangerous, but she didn't want to come to her senses.

They'd been staring for so long now she dared not move a single muscle. Her heart jerked with trepidation as she weighed the risks—stepping away and wasting this rare and precious moment with him versus staying locked in such intimate proximity that she could see the desire in his stare, hear his accelerated breathing, feel the heat of his body, so close but not quite close enough.

'Do it,' he said quietly, as if he'd read her mind.

Dazed by lust, her pulse roaring through her ears, Greer looked up from his lips, his intent stare luring her closer to reckless surrender. He looked as if he wanted to devour her. The door was closed but not locked. Anyone could walk in in search of them. But she couldn't find the energy to fight the forbidden temptation a second longer.

Ignoring the war between right and wrong, she stepped forward. Nate's hands found her waist as hers curved over his shoulders. He pulled her close. She surged up onto the balls of her feet. With a sigh of released anticipation that almost emerged as a groan, she pressed her lips to his, all the fight she'd battled for weeks draining away.

The thrill of her lips on his struck her like a blast, violent in its intensity. Every one of her former reservations popped like bubbles. Nate pressed one hand between her shoulder blades, his other cupping her face as he deepened the kiss. Greer yielded, her lips parting when his demanded it, her tongue sliding against his as he groaned, her backside hitting the edge of the counter as he stepped forward, his hard thigh between her legs causing all sorts of below-the-waist fluttering.

Panting hard, he broke free of their kiss to stare

down at her. 'I've waited so long for this,' he said, sliding his lips along her jaw to her earlobe so her body all but incinerated.

'Me too,' she said on a sigh as her head swam with dizzying exhilaration. She slid her fingers around the back of his neck and into his hair, needing to touch him to confirm he'd feel as good as she'd imagined.

'Can I touch you?' His stare blazed into hers, full of sexy confidence and undeniable promise.

'Yes,' she said, almost begging as she drew his mouth back to hers. Yes, yes, please, yes!

His hand snaked around her waist under her top, his fingertips dancing over the skin at the small of her back, setting off mini explosions along her tingling nerves. While their tongues duelled, their kisses ravenous, his other hand cupped her breast through her bra.

Greer choked out a strangled moan of euphoria. His touch felt so good. And so forbidden. She shouldn't be doing this. Not here. But she'd lost any ability to be rational. She could barely stand, kissing Nate was so hot.

Nate pulled back, watching her hungrily as his thumb rubbed back and forth across her peaked nipple sending tingles of delight radiating throughout her body. 'You are so sexy.'

'So are you.' She slid her hands down his muscular back to grip his waist to shunt his hips closer to where she ached to feel him, hard and thick behind the fly of his scrubs.

His desire for her darkened his expression so she barely recognised him. But she barely recognised herself. It had been so long since she'd felt so liberated. And wanted.

Nate cupped her backside and hoisted her onto the counter, stepping into the space between her spread thighs. 'I knew we'd be this good together.' He pressed his hips to hers, his erection between her legs so she rocked her hips and sighed. 'I knew it the first time we touched. When we shook hands on my first day.'

'This is crazy. We need to stop,' she said, in a desperate attempt to control the way he made her feel attractive and desirable. But in the same breath, she chased his lips with hers once more, seeking another life-affirming kiss as she held his waist so he couldn't escape.

'Not yet,' he said, trailing his lips and the wet tip of his tongue down the side of her neck. 'You're too sexy. You taste too good. Not yet…' He kissed her again, deeply, ravenously, clearly as on edge as Greer.

She slid her fingers through his hair, holding him close as their kisses deepened wildly, tongues surging together, their need escalating quickly out of control, as if they were each desperate and determined to squeeze in one more kiss before they'd have to break the spell and stop.

He slid her hips forwards to the edge of the counter, drawing them closer, grinding them together, the friction sublime. Simultaneously too much and too little. Greer moaned and tore her mouth from his, panting as she met his darkly aroused stare.

'Nate… We shouldn't be doing this,' she said in a half-hearted attempt to bring this madness to a close. But powerless to her own needs, she curled her fingers around the back of his neck and brought their lips back together, spread her thighs wider, craving more and more as pleasure erupted and engulfed her.

She was lost. Aroused and abandoned. Her need for him obliterating all else.

Nate groaned against her neck. 'I know… I just… I want you so badly.' His hips bucked against hers, sending more heat to pool in her pelvis. His hands cupped her face, fingers sliding into her hair, which must have been horribly dishevelled as he peered down at her, unmistakable craving on his face.

'Me too,' she admitted, kissing him again. Just one more kiss. Last time.

'Tell me to stop again and I will,' he said, bending his head to kiss her collarbone, her chest, down into her cleavage, groaning when he exposed a glimpse of black lace.

'I can't…' Her body molten with need, Greer struggled to breathe let alone speak or issue orders. Instead she kissed him again, determined this would be the very, very last time even as she slid her hands to his backside to press his hips closer so they moaned in unison at the gratifying contact.

But Nate clearly had more willpower than Greer. After one final searingly hot kiss where she feared she might never be able to stop this, that she might actually have sex with him, right there in the doctors' office, he pressed his forehead to hers and slid his hand from under her top.

'I've never wanted anyone as badly as I want you,' he said hoarsely, breathing hard as he eased his hips back, obviously mining impressive reserves of discipline.

Breathless, Greer could only stare and nod. Every inch of her body was alight with need. The past few wildly passionate minutes had shattered her every reservation about this reckless relationship. Her principles and professionalism were ground to dust. And she didn't care.

'I'm sorry. I shouldn't have done that,' she said, coming to some of her senses. Swallowing hard, Greer slid from the counter and ran a trembling hand through her tangled hair, trying to put herself back together.

'Don't apologise.' Nate helped, one hand still on her waist as he pushed her hair over her shoulder and smiled regretfully. 'That was even hotter than I'd imagined and I've been thinking about it a lot.'

Greer smiled, relieved that they'd got away with a serious lapse in judgement on her part. 'Still, we're at work.' Their shift didn't end for another hour. There would be more patients to see, and anyone could come in search of either of them and find them flushed and panting and still staring hungrily at each other. 'I should have controlled myself.'

'Well, I'm glad you couldn't.' Nate retrieved his name tag, which must have become dislodged during all the frantic kissing, from the floor and clipped it back on. 'How do I look?' he asked, catching his breath, a guilty but still hot smile tugging at his kiss-swollen mouth.

With her heart still tripping, Greer ran her fingers through his silky dark hair, straightening the strands. 'Like some woman has just ravaged you senseless in the doctors' office.'

'Cool.'

They smiled together, the tension breaking.

'Your coffee is probably cold,' she said, crossing her arms over her chest. 'Sorry about that.'

'Are you kidding?' he asked with an incredulous smile as fire once more flickered in his stare. 'Who needs coffee with you around?'

Greer smiled, pressing her lips together to hold in a giggle. She knew what he meant. Those kisses had rejuvenated her more effectively than an intravenous caffeine infusion.

'I need to get away from you,' Nate said, pressing his lips to her forehead, breathing into her hair. 'Get a hold of myself.'

Greer dragged in another shaky breath and stepped back, away from the temptation to kiss him again or keep touching him.

At the door, he paused and turned to shoot her another heated look. 'I don't think you need to worry about our date or be nervous. After that, I think our only problem will be avoiding setting Diamanto's ablaze.'

Greer nodded in agreement. 'If I don't see you before I head home, I'll see you Thursday evening,' she said, watching as he gave her one last smile then disappeared, leaving her to wonder how on earth she'd stop herself from ripping his clothes off the minute he knocked on her door for their date.

CHAPTER EIGHT

'So how come you're single?' Greer asked that Thursday evening, unable to put off the burning question a moment longer. She glanced guiltily around Diamanto's. They were one of only two couples still seated as the staff discreetly cleared up. But she didn't want the date to be over.

For the first time that evening, Nate's expression became guarded. 'My last relationship ended about a year ago.'

She nodded and twirled the stem of her near-empty wine glass, her gaze drawn to Nate's across the flickering candle flame at the centre of their table as it had been all evening while they'd talked about everything from their careers to the films and books they loved and their dream holiday destinations.

'We were only together three months,' he added, 'so it wasn't that serious.'

'Just didn't work out, huh?' she prompted, her curiosity burning bright. The closer the time came to leaving Diamanto's, the more nervous she felt, despite the lovely meal and abundant light and flirty conversation. Not to mention the heated looks. Because now she knew Nate was right. They were good together. Better than good. If they ever went further than some serious heavy petting, she had no doubt they'd be…utterly glorious.

'Kind of,' he said, his stare unflinching but no longer relaxed. 'It was good at the start. But after the first few weeks she became quite jealous. Not a great combination with a partner who works unpredictably long hours the way we do.'

Greer nodded in sympathy and understanding, aware that the same issues had arisen in her marriage. 'Did she…have any reason to be jealous?' Greer asked, her face hot because cheating or sneaking around was a definite trigger for her. Ironic, then, that she was sneaking around with Nate both at work and by hiding the relationship from Lily.

'I'm not a cheat, if that's what you're asking,' he said, his stare glittering. 'But yeah, she struggled with my close relationship to Maggie, Callum's mother.'

Greer winced. 'That's not good.' Especially when Nate was understandably supportive of his twin brother's widow and son.

Nate shrugged it off. 'Eventually we came to the joint realisation that it wasn't working out.

What about you?' he asked, changing the subject. 'Was there any cheating in your marriage?'

Greer shook her head, her throat tightening with shame as she reluctantly sipped the last of her wine. 'My ex always denied it, but that didn't stop me having plenty of suspicions over the years. My father cheated on my mother so I grew up witnessing the fallout of a trustless marriage. I guess that shaped me.'

'I'm sorry.'

Greer shrugged. 'I was determined that I would never tolerate that in my own relationships. But it's like you said. Our work is often unpredictable, our hours long, especially in surgery. My ex and I argued a lot, too. My suspicious nature combined with his propensity for emotional withdrawal when he felt challenged was not, it turned out, a match made in heaven.'

'How long were you married?' he said, his expression intensely watchful.

'Fourteen years. I think the final five were mainly for Lily's sake. We probably shouldn't have rushed to get married in the first place, but I got pregnant after a year of dating and on some level we obviously both thought it was the right thing to do.' One of her biggest fears about dating seriously again was that history might repeat itself. She might get it wrong again. Rush into something that wasn't right for her. Maybe that was why she'd put off dating for so long.

'Not that I regret it all, of course,' she continued. 'My marriage gave me my daughter and there were many happy times over the years, especially in the beginning.'

Nate nodded thoughtfully.

'Anyway…' Greer said, hating that they'd have to bring the date to an end. 'We should probably call it a night. If you haven't noticed, they're clearing up around us.'

'Yeah, I guess we should,' Nate said, standing and pulling out his wallet, clearly intent on paying the bill. 'Would you like to walk home? It's probably still warm out. I can walk you home then take the Tube.'

'Sure.' Greer nodded, slipping on her lightweight cardigan over the short-sleeved dress she'd worn, shivering slightly because Nate was so considerate and gentleman-like.

Now that the end of the evening was here, her nerves crept back. That kiss at the hospital had proved their sexual chemistry wasn't going to be a problem. And as much as she wanted him physically, she still had mental reservations. She didn't want to lead him on or for there to be any awkwardness at work. And if a kiss goodnight led to more, was she ready to be intimate with another man?

Nate insisted on paying for dinner, and as they left the restaurant, he reached for her hand, sliding his fingers between hers and tugging her close so they could walk hand in hand. Greer shuddered, both elated and unsettled by the illicit and intimate contact that still felt…forbidden. After weeks of keeping their flirtation a secret, the public gesture felt odd. But then he'd also given her the hottest kiss she'd experienced for years so there was no point denying how much she craved his touch.

'How was your first first date in years?' he asked, shooting her that sexy playful smile of his. 'Clearly you weren't put off by the cartoon socks.'

Greer laughed, her heart light. 'I had a lovely time. I was particularly thrilled to glimpse today's very appropriate socks—olives. Well chosen.'

'Thought you might like those,' he said, grinning.

'I'm impressed by your sock collection,' she said, to keep her mind off the dwindling minutes until they reached her place. 'You must own enough pairs to wear a different set every day, because, with the exception of my favourites, I've yet to see the same pair twice.'

'I'm glad to hear you've been keeping track.' He shot her another flirtatious look. Then his smile became tinged with sadness. 'Dylan started the trend. I was doing my Paediatrics rotation when he bought my first pair—pizza slices—as a Christmas gift. When I told him I'd worn them to work and one of the sick kids I'd treated that day had noticed them and smiled, he continued to buy more and more pairs, every birthday and Christmas. And sometimes just because he'd found a pair that stood out.'

Greer smiled, her heart thudding painfully for his enormous loss. 'You must miss him terribly. I can't even imagine what you and your family have been through.'

'I do miss him, of course,' Nate said, looking straight ahead as they walked. 'We were really close. His death left a massive hole in the family, not just in my life. That's why I try to spend time with Callum, so we can talk about Dylan whenever he wants. I'd hate for him to grow up feeling he couldn't mention his dad in case it upset people. Because his dad was amazing. I would never want him to forget that.'

'You're amazing, too,' she said, her throat tight with emotion. 'Callum's lucky to have such a dedicated uncle.'

'I don't know about that.' He looked straight ahead. 'Most of the time I just feel guilty. Dylan should be the one raising his son. He should be the one making memories, watching his football matches and talking about the issues at school.'

'I'm so sorry that he's gone,' Greer said, fighting the urge to hold him. But they weren't a couple. This was about lust and fun. About Greer finding her feet and jumping the first hurdle on her journey of self-rediscovery.

'Me too.' He glanced her way and shrugged. 'But that's why I haven't applied for a consultant job yet,' he said, volunteering information. 'I need to be good at my job, but I'm in no hurry to work longer hours or take on more responsibility. Callum is only eight and life is tough for kids these days. He needs positive role models now more than ever.'

Greer nodded, her heart pounding because he kept on showing her new parts of his personality and passions. And so far there was nothing she disliked. Not a single red flag to be seen.

They walked the last street in increasingly edgy silence. When they were standing on Greer's doorstep, Nate confidently tugged her hand, stepped close and dipped his head to hers, brushing a soft restrained kiss over her lips.

'I really enjoyed our date. Thanks for saying yes,' he said, his fingers holding hers. 'I wanted to ask you out the first day we met, as soon as I clocked the bare ring finger.'

Greer smiled, her heart leaping at his playfulness and confidence, her mind whirring suddenly because when she'd prepared for tonight, she hadn't planned to invite him in. But now she wanted more.

She slid her hand to his waist and pressed her mouth back to his, parting her lips when he kissed her harder, sliding her tongue against his, moaning when his arms encircled her, his hand pressed between her shoulder blades so there was no space between their bodies. Only heat and sparks and burning need she could no longer fight.

'Come inside,' she whispered after pulling back, her breathing tight and her heart racing.

Nate stared down at her, his eyes dark with desire, his erection a flicker against her stomach. 'Are you sure?'

'Yes.' Their chemistry was insane. She liked and respected Nate. They understood each other's priorities and she didn't have to worry about this becoming serious. It was just sex.

Before either of them could change their minds, she reached for his hand, turning to fumble for keys in her bag and unlock the outer door. Her flat was on the ground floor but they only made it inside the communal foyer before Nate pressed her up against the wall, his hands in her hair as he kissed her deeper, trailing his hot mouth down her neck.

'Greer,' he groaned. 'You are so sexy. I haven't been able to forget that kiss. Haven't stopped thinking about you since.'

'Come on,' she said, galvanised into action by the molten need making her legs unsteady.

Within seconds, they'd charged inside Greer's darkened flat, where he reached for her again. She shrugged off her cardigan, now too hot. His kisses grew more determined, his hands restlessly skimming her body, her breasts, waist, hips and backside through her clothes, his sexy groans unrestrained. Nate was honest about what he wanted and he wanted her.

All but levitating with lust, Greer tangled one hand in his hair while the other explored his bunched shoulder, his hard chest, the ridges of his steely abs and the long hard length of him behind his fly.

He groaned once more and she smiled. Every inch of him felt magnificent. A gloriously sexy man in his prime.

'Bedroom,' she said when they paused for breath. She led him down the hall and pushed open the door, grateful that she'd put her clothes in the laundry basket earlier rather than tossing them onto the bed or leaving them in a heap outside the shower.

'Tell me what you like,' he said, one arm banded around her waist as he kissed her while walking her backwards towards the bed, then pulled back, waiting.

What she liked? Greer's brain synapses shorted out; his demand was so sexy.

'You,' she said, embarrassed that she couldn't come up with something more sexually sophisticated like a favourite position or kink.

As if doused in chilly water, she stared up at him. 'Why? What do *you* like? Because… I haven't done this in a very long time.'

'I don't care.' He chased her lips with his, murmuring, 'That's hot. *You're* hot. And I want you, too.'

'But…' She swallowed again, already so turned on from his pretty simple touch, she felt sure she would reveal herself as too vanilla. Perhaps he expected dirty talk, some exotic position she'd never heard of. Perhaps he had a sexual fetish. She'd heard they were all the rage these days.

He gripped her face between his palms, his lips brushing hers. 'What's wrong, Greer? Tell me what has you suddenly overthinking this.'

Greer hesitated, her heartbeats now painful throbs in her chest. 'I'm worried there's a whole sexual subculture I knew nothing about. I'm worried that I'll disappoint you. I'm worried we won't click.'

Nate frowned and froze, staring wordlessly down at her for several long beats. Greer's stomach plummeted and her feet turned to stone, every doubt she'd thought she'd dismissed roaring back to life. Maybe she couldn't do this after all.

Nate breathed through the firestorm of his arousal burning him up, through the urge to kiss her, to tongue every inch of her body and pleasure her into incoherence. 'I'm sure there *is* a sexual subculture you know nothing about, but I'm sure I'm just as ignorant as you.'

He hadn't expected to be invited in tonight, but

he wasn't about to miss this opportunity. He felt feverish with wanting her, as if this moment—standing in the dark in her bedroom—had been building since the first time they met.

He pressed his lips back to hers, smiling into their kiss when she sagged against him with relief, peppering her face with more kisses. 'Just so we're on the same page, I'll tell you what I want.' He pulled back to stare at her. 'I want to kiss you and touch you and see you naked,' he said, sliding his palms up and down her bare arms. 'And you have my consent to do the same to me.'

She nodded, her hands sliding around his waist, her body restless against his as if, despite her wobble of confidence, she was as turned on as Nate. 'I do want.'

'Thank God.' Nate groaned, his lips desperately tracing her skin. 'I want to make you come and make you smile, make you laugh,' he continued, pressing her body against his. 'I want us to explore and enjoy each other and discover if this chemistry is as good as I know it's going to be.'

'Nate…' Greer gripped his upper arms, her doubts clearly appeased. 'I want that too.'

'So you'll tell me if I do something you don't like or don't want. And I'll do the same. Okay?' Nate cupped her breast with one hand while the other slid under her dress and slowly grazed her outer thigh.

'Yes.' She shifted against him, seeking friction. He ran his nose along her jaw to the place beneath her earlobe where her natural scent was strongest.

'You are the sexiest woman I've ever met, Greer,' he said. 'Just talking to you turns me on. I want you so badly, I'm scared this will be over too soon, before I've had a chance to do all the things I've imagined doing with you.'

Greer moaned, dropped her head back so his lips could glide wherever they wanted along her neck as he breathed her in and learned the sensitive places that made her sigh and twist her fingers in his hair.

'So are you still sure about this? Do you want to stop?' he asked, his fingers curling into the fabric of her dress at her waist as he held himself in check, waiting.

'No! I want to see you.' She slid her hands under his shirt where his skin was surely scalding hot, her hands roaming, his muscles tensing everywhere she touched as she shoved up his shirt and stared at his naked torso, her bottom lip trapped under her teeth.

Nate kissed her once more and reached for the zip at the back of her dress. The metallic scrape echoed in the silent room, the only other sound but for their increasingly ragged breathing. He pushed the dress from one shoulder, taking her bra strap too until he'd exposed her breast. Desperate to taste her and deliver on his promises, he leaned down and covered her nipple with his mouth, sucking and flicking it with the tip of his tongue so she gasped.

'Nate,' she said on a half-sob, watching him for a few seconds. Then with renewed determination, she pushed his shirt up, removing it, sliding the tip of her tongue over his chest, and up the side of his neck as if in retribution.

'Greer…' Nate crushed her semi-naked chest to his, skin to skin until he felt coated in the heady scent of her perfume. They kissed, intermittently breaking free for Greer to run her hands and her stare over his torso, for Nate to expose the other breast and take that nipple in his mouth until she moaned louder.

'You were right,' she said, sliding her arms free of her dress, allowing it to pool at her feet, removing her bra and kicking both items aside before stepping back into his arms. 'This is definitely about us and we are good together.'

'Better than good.' He smiled, satisfied, groaning when she kissed him deeply, her fingers unbuckling his belt and unbuttoning his jeans.

'Greer,' he said in warning as she stroked him through his boxers, her lips gliding along his collarbone.

Then her tongue headed south as she dropped to her knees and pushed his jeans over his hips, looking up at him with a feline smile.

'Great idea.' Nate reached for her elbows and

drew her to her feet, walking her back towards the bed, following her down when she lay in the middle. 'I want to taste you.'

Kicking off his shoes, he leaned over her, his hips between her spread thighs, and poured all the need that had been building these past few weeks into their frantic kisses.

She sighed as he kissed and licked a trail down her belly, sliding off her underwear as he went.

Pausing, he knelt between her legs and stared, his hands gliding up and down her thighs. 'You are so beautiful,' he choked out, arousal boiling his blood. 'Definitely worth the wait.'

'So are you,' she said when he stood and removed the rest of his clothes, and they stared at each other's naked bodies unashamedly.

He retrieved a condom from his wallet and then rejoined her on the bed, starting at her ankle and kissing a path up her leg until he was where he wanted to be.

'Yes,' she gasped as he covered her with his mouth, pleasuring her so all he heard were her cries and moans and chants of *yes*.

She speared her fingers through his hair, her moans building with every swipe of his tongue until she cried out and came, sobbing his name.

Before she could come down from the high, Nate tore into the condom and covered himself.

'Come here.' Greer reached for him, pulling

him into the cradle of her hips, gripping his waist with her thighs as he slowly slid into her warmth.

'Are you okay?' he asked, holding still, biting his tongue against the flood of pleasure radiating throughout his entire body.

'More than okay,' she said, smiling, brushing her lips over his, tilting her hips so he sank deeper and groaned against her neck. 'Let me go on top,' she whispered.

'No problem,' he said, gripping her waist to roll them, still locked together as one.

She was magnificent. Flushed from her orgasm, her hair dishevelled, her smile satisfied as she braced her hands on his chest. Staring down at him, she began to rock, riding him, her breaths panting as she found her rhythm and showed him her fearless passionate side, the one he'd been desperate to see.

'Still worried that we won't click,' he asked, one hand leaving her hips to cup her breast and toy with the nipple.

She laughed joyously, the sound shifting into a low moan as he thrust upwards when she rocked down. Nate found some hidden reserves of stamina, desperate for Greer to be in no doubt of their chemistry. Desperate to give her the time of her life so she had zero regrets.

With another broken cry she came again, tossing back her head to expose her neck. Nate sat up, crushed her in his arms, held her through every spasm and then finally let go, the high of being with Greer definitely worth the wait.

CHAPTER NINE

GREER'S HEAD GREW heavy on Nate's chest as she basked in the afterglow of astounding sex.

'How was that?' he asked, his voice smiling as he ran his fingertips lazily up and down her spine.

'Are you kidding?' she mumbled. 'I can't believe I waited so long…' She'd genuinely enjoyed every moment of their date. He'd made her laugh so many times over dinner and goodness knew it had been a long time since anyone apart from Lily and her girlfriends had done that. Not to mention the sex… She was definitely hung up on the sex.

He chuckled and reached for her hand, sliding his fingers between hers, the gesture so intimate—ridiculous she should think that after what had just happened—that her mind began to race.

They'd agreed this was casual, but did that mean they were done? She hadn't planned to invite him in tonight, but now that they'd slept together, she wanted to do it again. How could she not? Nate was a perfectly endowed god well acquainted with a woman's body.

'What happens now?' she asked, her hand on his abs so she felt him tense beneath her touch.

'Now I catch the Tube home,' he said, his fingers gliding through her tangled hair, 'and let you get some sleep.'

He pressed a kiss to the top of her head in another sweet gesture that left her even more panicked. Part of her didn't want him to leave. But nor did she really want him to stay the night. She needed to analyse every second of what had happened. Alone. To recall and overthink every word of conversation, every moaned utterance and desperate touch until it all made sense and she'd clarified exactly how she felt about it all.

It was one thing to want to bravely rediscover yourself. Another thing entirely to navigate the rules of casual sex with a younger man. Because as much as she still wanted him, she couldn't become too addicted.

She and Nate were at different stages of life. She'd done things—marriage, a child—that he still had ahead of him. She wouldn't lead him on, not when this could never be a serious or long-term thing.

'Okay,' she said, unmoving, because part of her wanted him for a little longer.

'I'm taking Callum to the dentist first thing tomorrow,' Nate explained, 'because Maggie has an early start at work. Then dropping him at school after his appointment.'

Greer nodded, grateful that Nate too had obligations. She'd planned to organise Lily's surprise eighteenth birthday party tomorrow. Hire caterers, message all of Lily's friends, order a couple of cases of champagne.

'Has your sister-in-law begun dating again?' she asked, her mind returning to their earlier conversation in the restaurant. The one where he'd expressed guilt that it was him and not Dylan parenting Callum.

'Yeah, a bit.' Nate's slow even breaths stalled. 'Don't think she's met anyone serious though.'

'It's great that you help out with childcare,' Greer said, picking up on a feeling that he was hiding something. That she'd touched a nerve earlier and again just now.

Or maybe he simply wanted to leave now that the sex was over.

'I do it for Dylan, mainly,' he said quietly. 'I've never really wanted kids of my own, but if I had one and the roles were reversed, if it was my child left fatherless, I'd want my child to know their uncle.'

'Of course,' Greer said, a part of her needing him to be a bit less wonderful. But it was obviously just the sex talking. She'd left it too long and now she feared she'd want more and more despite her current massive hangover. It had been that good.

'For what it's worth,' she said, finally raising her head to look at him, 'I think you're doing your brother proud.'

Rather than take her compliment, he froze, his body tensing under hers. Sensing his discomfort, Greer sat up, drawing the sheet up to cover her nakedness. Nate rose too, turning away from her to sit on the edge of the bed, his forearms braced on his thighs.

'I'm not so sure about that,' he muttered, reaching for his boxers from the floor before pulling them on.

What? This wasn't the confident, self-assured man she'd come to know.

'Why not?' Greer asked, shivering from the sudden chill in the atmosphere.

'I'm a doctor,' he said, standing and pulling on his jeans with hurried movements, making all her lovely post-orgasm endorphins drain away. 'I of all people should have spotted the signs of Dylan's illness sooner, don't you think?'

'No, I don't. You weren't *his* doctor. It wasn't your fault.' Her voice was flat because she wasn't sure he was even listening. This conversation was obviously a trigger for him. He couldn't seem to get dressed quickly enough.

He smiled mirthlessly, shaking his head. 'Technically you're right, but that doesn't change the facts that by the time he sought help for his symptoms, he already had stage four disease and was dead within a year.'

He disappeared for a second inside his shirt. When his head emerged, he'd withdrawn behind the determined expression of his. 'It makes no difference now, but there's a part of me that can't help but wonder if I'd been less self-absorbed, less busy chasing the next job and passing the next exam, I might have noticed something was wrong with my twin brother. Been there for him when he needed me most, when it might have made a difference.'

Greer nodded, sadly, knowing nothing she said would likely change Nate's flawed thinking or the way he felt irrationally responsible for his brother. And it wasn't her place to try and fix Nate. He was a smart man. He'd figure this out for himself in time.

And their…relationship was just a bit of fun. A brief fling at best.

'I'm sorry that's the way you feel,' she said quietly. 'Is that why you need to be good at your job? To prove something to yourself?'

Nate stared. 'You know, up until this moment, I've always admired your directness. But yes, the part of me that let him down, the part that's scared to forget Dylan, needs to be good at my job. I couldn't help him but maybe I can help others.'

Greer glanced down, ashamed that she'd overstepped the mark. 'Sorry. It's none of my business.'

Uncertain how to proceed, she watched him pull on his socks. Maybe she should end things on a high. Send him off with a '*thanks for the date, for the orgasms, but let's resume business as usual*'. Only the pinch of disappointment in her stomach told her she wanted more.

'I'm going to head out.' He looked up and levelled his guilty but guarded stare on her as if waiting for more trite advice. When she stayed silent, merely nodding that she'd heard, he braced his hands on the bed and leaned over her, kissing her lips. 'Despite this last conversation, I had a great time tonight.'

'Me too,' Greer said, feeling irrationally hurt that he was leaving on a sour note. 'I'll see you out.' She flung off the sheet, rose from the bed and donned her robe, which had been hanging on the back of the bedroom door.

When she looked up from tying the belt around her waist, Nate's stare blazed with hunger.

'I want you again,' he said starkly but unmoving, as if he now resented the hold she might have over him.

'I thought you were leaving,' she replied, fresh heat sliding through her limbs to settle in her core, because she wanted him too. One time wasn't enough. Not when they'd clicked so magnificently.

Nate prowled closer, his stare locked to hers. 'I only had one condom,' he said, scrubbing a hand over his face. 'And you haven't invited me to stay the night.'

She squared her shoulders, determined to set some boundaries. 'Maybe now is a good time to address our expectations for this.'

He nodded, tension pursing his sexy mouth. 'I want more than a one-time thing. I'd like to see you again. What do you want?'

'So I'd be your boss with benefits?' she asked, liking the idea more than she'd imagined possible. 'I can handle that.' Why not? Nate was fun and respectful and the sex… How had she gone without for so long?

A hint of amusement tugged at his lips. 'If you like.'

'Obviously that's all it can be: a fling,' she pointed out, because Nate could have his pick of women his own age and Greer wasn't ready for a real relationship. 'Neither of us wants anything serious.'

She wasn't sure she ever wanted to be married again. In fact, the idea of being so romantically vulnerable again made her want to change her mind, end this now before either of them could get hurt.

'Whatever you want, Greer.' He stepped closer

still, his gaze flicking to her lips so her heart galloped, her wants a confusing jumble among her desires.

'Lily's home from France in nine days,' she said, breathlessly, deciding that might be a good place to draw the line. 'When she's home, I won't really have time for sneaking around or keeping secrets. We'll be preparing for her move to Manchester.'

'Okay,' he said, his expression unreadable. If he was disappointed, he kept it hidden.

Greer dragged in a shaky relieved breath at such smoothly negotiated terms. 'In that case, I'll buy a jumbo box of condoms tomorrow,' she said, lingering fear forcing her not to reach for him, not to kiss him, to drop to her knees and take him into her mouth until he growled her name and forgave her for overstepping the mark before.

His face slowly split into a sexy smile. 'Good idea. I will too.'

He reached for her waist, but she ducked away, shooting him her best seductive look. She left the bedroom and breezed her way down the hall to the front door, her silky robe billowing.

This, him leaving, them both hungry for more, was the perfect finale to their date. She could come to terms with her reawakened physical desires while sending the right message that they shouldn't get too used to each other because this had temporary stamped all over it.

She opened the flat door and stepped aside while he put on his shoes. Looking up, his stare darkening, he closed the distance, scooped one arm around her waist and kissed her hard and deeply, pressing her against the wall with his hips.

Instantly and impossibly needy given the two orgasms she'd had, she clung to his shoulders, kissing him back, her resolve forgotten. Hooking one leg around his thigh so his hardness prodded between her legs and he groaned into their kiss.

He pulled back, panting. 'Do you have plans for the weekend?' His hand cupped her backside, holding their hips snug as they rocked together teasingly, mini aftershocks of pleasure spiralling out from her core.

Greer shook her head, too turned on from the heat of that kiss and the possessive look in his eyes to make any sense or put up another fight.

'Can I see you?' He pushed her hair back from her flushed face, the pad of his thumb tracing her cheekbone as his stare turned a little vulnerable.

'Okay,' she said. 'I'll meet you in Covent Garden, at the Seven Dials monument, Saturday afternoon, four p.m.'

A small satisfied smile tugged the corners of his mouth, a mouth that had wreaked sublime havoc on every part of her body. 'See you there.'

With a final swift kiss, he released her and

stepped out into the foyer. 'Sleep well, Greer.' Then he turned and left.

'You too,' she called, closing the door before he disappeared out onto the street, when all she really wanted to do was watch him until the last minute, a dreamy smile on her face.

But just because she'd had life-altering sex didn't mean she could forget herself. She still needed to be professional at work. Her priority was still her daughter. They could enjoy a few stolen moments until Lily arrived home but beyond that it wouldn't do to become addicted to him or forget that long term, for many reasons, they were a highly unlikely match.

CHAPTER TEN

IT HAD BEEN easy to swap his Sunday early shift with one of the other emergency medicine registrars so Nate could work the Friday night shift with Greer. Not that he'd told Greer his plans or seen her since he began the shift an hour ago. But this way, he could enjoy their second date Saturday afternoon without having to think about an early start the next day.

He'd just finished helping one of the junior doctors to reduce a dislocated shoulder and was checking some results at the computer terminal, when Greer appeared from one of the patient bays.

Dressed in their usual navy scrubs, her dark hair, which had been sexily dishevelled the last time he'd seen her, was pulled back in a neat ponytail. Her eyes lit up when she saw him, her ready smile falling as the shock and delight drained away and she quickly glanced around the department in case someone might be looking.

'What are you doing here?' she asked in a suspicious whisper, taking the seat beside his and trying to act normal. But her cheeks flushed as if she was recalling the last time they'd seen each other. The things they'd done to each other. The way that they'd slotted so perfectly together in the bedroom. For the entire journey home on the Tube, Nate had cursed his lack of preparation on the condom front.

'I swapped shifts with Dr Beynon,' he said, his heart pounding and his smile uncontrollable. 'Turns out I've developed rather an addiction to night shifts recently.'

And also an addiction to Greer. Thursday night had been… Wow! And right up until the moment where she'd prodded him to talk about Dylan, he hadn't wanted to leave. He'd had such an amazing night, had been half sex-comatosed, that he'd relaxed too much. Let his guard slip so when she'd probed, he'd revealed something he might otherwise have kept to himself. But he needed to be careful. If this was only casual, if they had only a matter of days left to enjoy each other, he needn't tell her his other guilty secret.

'You ought to see a doctor for that,' she quipped, flashing him a playful smile. 'But as you're here, you can take the ingrowing toenail in bay two.' She cast him a straight-faced look.

'No problem.' Nate grinned, gratified to have her play with him after his minor freak-out Thursday night. That, despite their hot night together and the subsequent rather clinical discussion of their romantic expectations, he still had the power to affect her and vice versa.

Just then, before he could ask her if she'd thought of him after he'd left her place, the way he'd obsessed over her, Michelle, one of the senior nurses, appeared.

'Dr Thorn, thanks for the books,' she said. 'I really appreciate it.'

'Oh, no problem, Michelle,' Greer replied. 'I hope your son finds them helpful. Lily no longer has any use for them so they might as well go to someone else.'

'I'm sure he will,' Michelle said. 'Maths is his least favourite subject but he needs to pass the A level next year if he's hoping to study engineering.'

Greer smiled warmly and Michelle rushed off to answer a call buzzer. Nate waited until she looked up at him then raised his eyebrows questioningly.

'I gave Michelle Lily's study guides for her son who is in lower sixth.' She touched the mouse on the desk to wake up the computer, before logging in, ignoring Nate, who continued to stare, mesmerised.

'That was very thoughtful of you,' he said, his gaze tracing her profile, the elegant slope of her neck, a place he'd explored with his lips and tongue until she'd moaned.

Greer gave so much of herself to others, through her job, to her colleagues, to Lily. Nate couldn't help but wonder what she needed for herself. And with that question came stirrings of doubt. He'd agreed to a casual fling. That was the safest option, the one Greer wanted, too. But a part of him was already addicted to her physically. Addicted to her quiet strength. Her sometimes dry sense of humour. Her unguarded smile and joyously throaty laugh.

'What?' she asked, because he was still staring.

Nate shrugged. 'I just like that you know who you are. How you handle things. It's…attractive,' he whispered the final word and her gaze darted around the department once more.

'Stop,' she said, a small knowing smile tugging at the corner of her mouth. 'Go and discharge that ingrowing toenail if you've got nothing better to do.'

'Whatever you say, Dr Thorn.' He stood, and paused, stooping to add another playful whisper. 'I love it when you boss me around.' He made his way towards the patient, her startled gasp ringing in his ears. He unleashed a satisfied grin. It was good to know that, after their incredible date, he still had the power to surprise her.

Greer watched Nate walk away, her heart pounding erratically. His tall swagger, the clench of his gorgeous backside, the way he'd whispered that last comment close enough that his warm breath had slid down her neck like honey, igniting her erogenous zones… She licked her lips and released a happy sigh, snapping out of her dreamy state when Nate was intercepted by Kaz, one of the junior doctors working the shift.

'Nate, can I ask you a question?' Kaz said, blinking up at him with obvious awe.

'Of course. Any time,' he replied, glancing down at the department's tablet Kaz held.

Greer stopped listening, trying to focus on the computer screen, on the patient notes she was typing up, but her gaze kept returning to Nate and Kaz, who were now side by side, each looking at the tablet while they talked.

Greer half listened, half squirmed, catching phrases that made it obvious they were discussing a patient…basal crepitations…congestive cardiac failure…diuretics… Maybe it was in Greer's imagination that Kaz, a pretty twenty-something, was standing a little too close to Nate. Smiling a little too much. Nodding too enthusiastically when Nate advised her on appropriate tests and a management plan.

Feeling uncomfortable spying and unsettled by the intensity of her feelings of jealousy, Greer typed a few more lines of her notes. But when she looked up again, Kaz and Nate were still talking. Only now Kaz wore a wide smile, the tablet clasped to her chest, the patient discussion clearly over.

'Thanks so much for your help,' Kaz gushed on a tinkle of nervous laughter. 'I completely understand now that you've explained it. I actually like working with you. The other registrars always act too busy for my silly questions.' Kaz smiled and twirled the end of her long ponytail.

Sharp stabs of jealousy pricked Greer's skin, leaving her hot and itchy. It was irrational. Greer had no claim to Nate. They weren't a couple. They weren't seriously dating. She'd even voiced as much the night before when she'd insisted all it could be was a fling. But maybe because Kaz was so much more suited to Nate, age-wise, Greer couldn't seem to dismiss her feelings as easily as she would have liked.

'No worries,' Nate said. 'Come find me later when you have the results back, yeah?' He stepped back, glancing over Kaz's shoulder to see Greer watching the interaction.

Mortified, she ducked her head, resumed her typing, aware of Kaz departing. Hopefully Nate would continue towards the ingrowing-toenail patient and Greer could pull herself together in peace.

No such luck.

'Hey, you okay?' Nate asked from beside her.

Greer finished typing her sentence then looked up from the screen. 'Of course.'

Of course Nate would be popular with the ladies. He was gorgeous and evolved and fun. Not that in answering Kaz's patient query he'd done anything more than his job. But Greer couldn't seem to move past her instantaneous but irrational spike of possessiveness.

'Did you send the toenail home?' she asked coolly, desperately trying to hide her uncertainty and embarrassment that she'd not only been listening in to his conversation but also gone right back to a place of distrust, a pathway she knew well.

'I'm on my way now,' he said, a small frown tugging at his mouth as he hesitated, obviously eager to say more or call Greer out on her attitude.

'Great,' she said, turning back to the screen as shameful heat blazed through her. Was she really pulling rank with Nate just to manage her unexpected feelings of jealousy? When she'd insisted this was only a fling?

Just then, before she could examine her behaviour more closely, the code blue alarm sounded. Greer ran to Resuscitation, aware that Nate followed close behind.

'Suspected ectopic pregnancy,' Michelle said as the nurses hurriedly prepared for the emergency admission. 'Patient twelve weeks gestation, first pregnancy confirmed by her general practitioner.'

'Call the obstetrics registrar,' Nate instructed Kaz, who'd also responded to the emergency alarm. 'We'll need cross-match for a transfusion just in case and blood work in preparation that the patient needs surgery.'

There was no time for Greer to rationalise her earlier envy. With an emergency like this it was all hands on deck. Within seconds, the patient was wheeled through the doors from the ambulance bay, and everyone present sprang into action.

'Latest blood pressure one hundred over sixty,' the paramedic said, stepping back from the stretcher to give the team access.

While Kaz drew blood to cross-match for a transfusion if required, Nate quickly examined the patient. Greer observed her vital signs. She had tachycardia and hypotension. With a history of abdominal pain and positive pregnancy test, the signs added up to a ruptured ectopic pregnancy and internal bleeding.

'Helen, we're going to run some tests, okay?' Nate said to the patient while Greer inserted a second intravenous cannula.

'Let's get more fluids going,' Nate said to Michelle, who hurried to start a second intravenous infusion of saline.

'Have you had any vaginal bleeding?' Greer asked the young woman, to which Helen nodded.

'A little,' she said shakily, her voice thick with

tears. 'Then the pain started. It got so bad that I fainted, so my partner called the ambulance.'

Having examined the woman's abdomen, Nate glanced at Greer, their stares meeting. 'She's tender in the supra-pubic region with guarding,' he said, describing definite signs of peritonitis.

'Helen,' Greer said, 'we need to perform an ultrasound scan. You have signs of internal bleeding, so we just need to see what's going on.'

The woman nodded tearfully and Nate reached for the mobile ultrasound they kept in Resus. He squirted gel onto the end of the probe, sliding it over her lower abdomen where the woman was tender.

Greer stood beside him so they could each see the screen. While Nate oriented himself, adjusting the resolution of the grainy scan images, Kaz approached.

'Obstetrics are on their way,' she said.

Greer nodded. 'Thanks. Can you chase up the urgent blood results, plcase?'

'There's free fluid in the pouch of Douglas,' Nate told Greer, pointing out what they'd already suspected. There was some internal bleeding causing some of Helen's symptoms.

'I agree,' she said, watching over his shoulder as Nate repositioned the probe.

He paused, the image on the screen showing Greer the empty uterine cavity. He looked up, their eyes meeting. She gave a tiny nod, acknowledging the significance of the finding: there was no embryo inside the uterus.

Nate shifted the probe again towards the right fallopian tube and ovary.

'What are you seeing?' Greer asked him, taking the moment to test his clinical acumen.

'There's a four-centimetre adnexal mass here,' he said, once more meeting Greer's stare.

Greer gave a small nod, silently communicating that they were on the same page when it came to their clinical suspicions. Evidence of internal bleeding and a mass involving the right fallopian tube most likely represented a ruptured ectopic pregnancy.

As Nate finished the scan, and gently wiped the gel from Helen's abdomen, Greer gave him an encouraging nod, letting him know she agreed with his diagnosis and was there to support him when it came to breaking the sad news to the patient.

'We've asked our colleague from Obs and Gynae to see you, Helen,' Nate said. 'Our concern is that the pregnancy is ectopic. It looks like the embryo implanted outside the womb in the fallopian tube and as it's grown, it's ruptured. You have some internal bleeding, so you'll most likely need surgery, I'm afraid. Did your partner come with you?'

Helen nodded, a confused frown on her face. 'He's outside calling our parents.'

From beside him, Greer added, 'Unfortunately, there's nothing we can do to save the embryo. I'm so sorry.'

Tears seeped from the corners of Helen's eyes. 'Can't we wait and see what happens?'

'We'll take advice from the specialist who is on his way,' Nate said, 'but you're already bleeding internally so the risk of further bleeding is high. Your blood pressure is low, so waiting might not be an option, I'm afraid. We have to put your safety first.'

The patient nodded bravely and Nate touched her shoulder. 'I'll talk to your partner and send him in to be with you while we wait for the obstetrician.'

'Thank you,' Helen said, obviously in shock.

Greer followed Nate away from the bedside, speaking in a hushed voice. 'I'll check the blood work and wait for the obstetrics' reg. Why don't you get what additional history you can from the partner?'

He nodded distractedly and Greer's empathy swelled. The job of breaking bad news like this was never easy. But it was an inevitable part of their work.

'You did good,' Greer said, resisting the urge to touch his arm. 'You know where I am if you need me.'

And then she walked off, determined to stay busy for the rest of the night. Because busy meant there'd be no time to question what she was doing with Nate or how inappropriate it was on multiple levels. No time to examine her jealousy and what it meant. No time to conclude that she was playing with fire and needed to be very careful so no one got hurt.

CHAPTER ELEVEN

BY FIVE IN the morning, Greer had barely seen Nate. She'd been granted her wish. A constant stream of walking wounded and inebriated patients had kept all three doctors on duty occupied. But after checking in with Kaz, who was in the process of assessing a woman with a minor scald, Greer finally sloped off to the doctors' room to freshen up and rehydrate.

She downed half a bottle of water and had just emerged from the bathroom, where she'd cleaned her teeth, brushed her hair and splashed cold water on her face, when Nate appeared, obviously also headed for the office.

He came to a sudden halt. 'Hi.' There was a hint of a smile in his eyes but also a wariness for which she was responsible after her coolness earlier.

'How's it going out there?' she asked, trying to act normal as she stashed her bag in the lockers.

'It's quietening down,' he said with a small frown. 'How about your end?'

'Same. I planned on grabbing a quick coffee. Want to join me?'

'What's going on, Greer?' he asked in an exasperated tone of voice. 'I saw you watching me earlier with the junior. Now you're acting distant.'

Flushing, Greer swallowed and glanced down at her feet, scuffing her toe over the linoleum. 'Nothing is going on. I just… I didn't mean to watch you. It struck me that you and Kaz look very good together.'

'Are you jealous?' he asked, his frown deepening as if he was stunned and disappointed rather than flattered.

'No. I mean she was so obviously flirting with you, which was hard to watch.' Greer looked away, her entire body flushing, hating how uncertain she now felt of Nate in the wake of her jealousy.

Rather than respond, Nate quickly scanned the empty corridor and then took her arm and led her into the on-call room a few doors down from the doctors' office.

'What are you doing?' Greer asked, her pulse so fast it hummed in her head. They couldn't be caught together in here.

'This.' He cupped her face and fiercely kissed her, pressing her back against the closed door.

Unable to stop herself because it felt like an age since they'd kissed goodnight yesterday, Greer kissed him back, her lips parting, her tongue stroking his, her hands gripping his waist to drag him close so his hard body pressed against hers from chest to thigh until her doubts fell silent.

'I've waited all night to do that,' he said when he pulled back, breathless, dragging his lips over her jaw, her cheek, pressing kisses to her eyelids. His lips left her skin and she opened her eyes to see desire on his face but also the return of his irritation. 'I don't care how we looked together, Greer. I didn't flirt back. I don't deserve the cold shoulder. You have nothing to be jealous about.'

Greer nodded, her body aflame from both Nate's touch and her confusion. 'I… I know.'

'It was nothing,' he emphasised. 'A harmless comment I wouldn't have given a second thought but for the look on your face.'

As if he couldn't stop touching her despite his annoyance, he tunnelled his fingers into her hair. 'I've thought about you constantly since I left your place last night. I've waited all night for the chance to kiss you. I know you have trust issues, but it was one work-related conversation.'

She nodded again, her throat tight. 'I'm sorry.'

His frustrated stare searched hers. 'Have you even thought about me at all since last night?'

'Of course I have,' she said, her fingers clenching at his waist. 'I woke up thinking about you. I could barely walk. I've struggled to think about anything else but what happened last night, anything but you and how you made me feel.'

As if satisfied with her answer, Nate groaned and kissed her again. More desperately this time, as if trying to prove her jealousy was unfounded. Greer clung to him, uncaring that they might be discovered together, eager to show him that her desperation matched his.

'Nate,' she said when he pulled back from their kiss. She dropped her head back against the door, absorbing every sensation of his touch: his hot breath on her neck, the scrape of his stubble against her skin, his wandering hand delving under her top to cup her breast as if he couldn't stop himself.

'Tell me how I made you feel,' he demanded, peering down at her while he stroked her nipple.

'Alive,' she said on a gasp, so instantly turned on, she forgot about the world beyond this room. 'Liberated. Desired. Accepted for being myself.' Unwilling to drown in desire alone, Greer cupped his erection, stroking him through his trousers.

His lips returned to hers, nibbling, tasting, buzzing as he released an agonised groan of pent-up need. 'I want you,' he said, his lips grazing her jaw and the side of her neck. 'I can't stop wanting you. I can't wait until this afternoon when I'll see you again.'

Mindless from pleasure, Greer fumbled at her back for the door lock and gave it a twist.

Nate pulled back, his aroused stare full of questions.

'I want you too,' she said, her throat tight. 'I wanted you last night when I was alone and again when I woke up this morning. I wanted you the minute I saw you tonight.'

Nate pressed his forehead to hers, breathing hard as if trying to pull himself together.

Greer slipped her fingers into her pocket and pulled out the condom she'd stashed there earlier in the bathroom, pressing it into his hand. 'I thought we needed to be better prepared after last night. I've stashed condoms all over my flat. We'll have to use them all before Lily gets home, don't want her traumatised if she finds one.'

There was just enough light entering through the crack under the door to witness the surprise and then growing arousal on his face as he considered her suggestion. 'That is the best plan I've ever heard,' he said, settling his lips over hers once more, his tongue surging and retreating, his kisses deepening until she was dizzily high.

'Hurry,' she said, kicking off her shoes, shoving down her trousers and underwear. 'We might not have much time.'

'I don't want to hurry,' Nate said with a trace of a sexy smile. He braced one hand on the door above her shoulder, kissed her again, his other hand sliding between her legs where she was beyond ready for him.

In near total darkness, all she could see was the gleam of his eyes as they kissed and stroked each other into a frenzy of need. Greer bit back every moan that wanted to escape and swallowed every gasp. But his touch stoked her entire body, heat racing along every nerve as he stroked her clit and watched her increasingly desperate reactions.

When he raised the hem of her top and peeled down the cup of her bra to suck her nipple, Greer shattered, her orgasm weakening her legs as she covered her mouth to hold in her cries so no one passing would hear.

Then he picked her up, deposited her backside on the room's desk and shoved down his clothing to put on the condom.

'What are you doing to me?' he asked rhetorically, kissing her again and again so she couldn't possibly respond even if she'd had the answer. Because whatever it was, he was doing it to her too.

Greer wrapped her legs around his hips and held his shoulders as he slid her to the edge of the desk and slowly pushed inside her and then froze for a second, each panting and staring as if in wonder.

'This was your idea,' she said, sliding her fingers through his hair. 'For me it's a definite disciplinary action.' But she couldn't seem to find the energy to stop or care.

'Only if we get caught,' he said, his fingers rubbing over her still exposed nipple as he started to thrust. 'Do you want to stop?'

'No!'

He smiled, his lips recaptured hers, his tempo building as their tongues surged together wildly. Greer crossed her ankles and clung to his shoulders, lost to everything but the way he and this fling made her feel free and powerful and reborn. Stronger and ready to face whatever her future held. There was life after divorce. Euphoric, wonderful life.

She tore her mouth from his as her second orgasm hit, staring into his eyes as wave after wave stole her breath and her mental capacity so she was pure joyous abandon.

'Greer,' he groaned, crushing her to his chest as he bucked and stiffened and breathed heavily against the side of her neck, holding her tight, their hearts thudding side by side.

After, they held each other in the dark for what felt like long minutes, their breaths easing.

'You okay?' he asked eventually, cupping her face, brushing her lips with his in that tender way.

Greer nodded, choked, and he withdrew. Finding a box of tissues on the desk, he dealt with the condom and pulled up his clothes. Greer held his waist, uncertain she'd be able to stand. That was when the giggles began.

'I can't believe we just did that,' she said from behind her hand.

Nate pressed his lips to her forehead. 'I can't

believe how incredibly sexy you are. I'm only human.'

He took her hands as she slid from the desk, stooping to collect her clothing from the floor.

'Nate, I'm sorry about earlier. I'm ashamed of how easily I slipped into old habits.'

He held out her clothes, then gripped the back of her neck and pressed his lips to her forehead. 'It's okay. We all have our triggers.'

Nodding, Greer pulled on her underwear and then her scrubs. 'You leave first,' she told him, slipping on her shoes. 'If the corridor is clear, tap the door twice and walk away. I'll wait a minute and follow.'

'Whatever you say, boss.' Nate snaked an arm around her waist, kissing her again. 'Just one more kiss to tide me over until this afternoon.'

'You might want to find a mirror,' she said when he released her, his light-hearted jibe touching a guilty nerve. 'Check that you're presentable.'

He smiled. 'If I look a fraction as good as I feel I'll be a happy man. If I don't see you before you leave, I'll see you later in Covent Garden.'

Greer nodded, watched him leave, heard his two taps on the door, her heart surging in her chest. As she waited a moment, her high drained away. That was the hottest, most reckless thing she'd ever done. Not that she had a single regret beyond her silly jealousy.

But as she straightened her hair, her stomach quivering, only now in trepidation, not pleasure, she lectured herself to calm down. She needed to be careful with Nate. Just because he made her feel twenty-something again, she wasn't. This fling was fun, but it could never turn into a serious relationship. Greer clearly wasn't ready for that and Nate needed someone his own age, someone without an ex-husband and a teenaged daughter. Someone without Greer's emotional baggage.

Deciding she had nothing to fear as long as she reined in her possessiveness and stuck to the deadline they'd set, she returned to the emergency department to see if any new patients had arrived.

CHAPTER TWELVE

LATER THAT MORNING, after watching Callum's football match, Nate used the key Maggie had given him to unlock her front door, allowing Callum to enter ahead of him.

'Don't forget to take off your muddy boots,' he told the boy. 'Remember the trouble I got into last time you forgot.'

Callum dutifully did as he was told, shouting a quick hello to his mother before running into the back garden where he'd recently discovered tadpoles in their small ornamental pond.

Nate headed for the kitchen and dropped Callum's bag in front of the washing machine. 'Hi,' he said to Maggie, who came in through the back door carrying a laundry basket.

'Did his team win?' Maggie asked, flicking on the kettle and reaching for a couple of mugs from the wall cupboard.

'Lost, two goals to one,' Nate replied, 'but, to be honest, he seemed more upset that the tadpoles might have grown legs while he was out.'

Maggie smiled indulgently and said, 'Coffee?' She added two heaped teaspoons to her mug and glanced up at Nate expectantly.

'No, thanks. I don't have time.'

'You sure? You look tired.'

'I worked the night shift last night.' Surviving on caffeine, the tepid shower he'd grabbed at the hospital before he'd left and the anticipation of his date with Greer later, Nate planned to forgo sleep today.

Maggie's eyes widened with shock. 'Then go home and sleep. What are you doing watching Callum's football match?'

'I promised him,' he said, simply. 'And I'm actually heading back out later. I'm meeting someone. I um…have a date.'

Maggie's eyes rounded with surprised delight. 'A date? That's awesome. Who is she?'

Nate shrugged, uncomfortable to discuss this with her. Not because of the mistake they'd made by sleeping together—that was in the past—but because he didn't want to upset his sister-in-law, who, despite going on a couple of token dates this summer, was still grieving Dylan's loss.

'Just someone from work,' he said, momentarily reliving that hot quickie in the staff on-call room. 'It's early days.'

Although all his instincts about Greer had proved accurate. They had fun together, respected each other, aside from her minor wobble last night. And the sex *was* explosive. She was…incredible. Although that moment of distrust had given him pause. If Greer was jealous over a harmless conversation, how would she react to his relationship with Maggie once he told her about their mistake?

'But…' Maggie said, peering at him over the rim of her mug, waiting for more.

'But, yeah… I really like her.' So much so that ever since she'd suggested the expiry date when Lily returned home, he'd been racking his brains for ways he could persuade her to extend their fling. He understood that her daughter was her priority, but why end a good thing if it was working? Surely Greer would agree and they could be discreet.

'So what's she like?' Maggie pushed, her eyes only slightly shiny with repressed emotion.

Nate took a deep breath, grateful to have someone he could tell about Greer, because Dylan would have been his first choice. 'She's smart and kind and…you know, all the things.'

Career-driven, self-assured with a great sense of humour. And so sexy he couldn't think straight when they were together.

'How does she feel about you?' Maggie asked, sliding onto a bar stool and blowing the surface of her drink to cool it.

Nate shrugged one shoulder, not sure he wanted to know that Greer saw him only as a good time for now, because his feelings for her were, he suspected, so much more…complex. Why else would he have reacted so viscerally to her jealousy? 'It's going in the right direction for now.'

He understood her reservations about their age gap. Knew that her divorce and her past had impacted her ability to trust men. But right then, he couldn't imagine them simply walking away from this in a few days' time. But if he wanted Greer for more than a fling, that came with a big risk. He'd have to tell her about Maggie and risk that she'd react negatively like his ex and walk away.

Maggie nodded knowingly. 'Well, don't play it too cool, will you? A woman likes to know she's exceptional.'

'Yeah…' Nate half-heartedly agreed, not because Greer wasn't exceptional—she most definitely was—but because where he feared his addiction to Greer was growing stronger day by day, she was already plotting the end of them. Maybe her trust issues were bigger than he'd realised.

'Have you…discussed your pasts?' Maggie asked carefully.

'Yeah, a bit. I mean, she's divorced so…' Nate dragged in a sigh. 'But I haven't told her everything.'

And the longer he kept his secret from Greer,

the harder it was to just casually mention it, especially after last night. He didn't want it to become an issue between them, though. If there was any chance she might want to keep seeing him after Lily returned home, he'd have to tell her soon. Then again, if she saw no future in their relationship, he could keep his secret to himself.

Maggie nodded, looking guilty. 'I know you had that bad experience with Mia, but maybe this time it will be different.'

He nodded again, his doubts unfurling. He'd never given Greer any reason not to trust him. She was a mature woman who knew her own mind and was comfortable in her own skin. Two things he really admired about her. But, like his ex, she might well care about his close relationship with his sister-in-law once she knew the whole story.

At that moment, Callum ran inside. 'Uncle Nate, Mum, come see. One of the tadpoles has turned into a frog.' He took Nate's hand and led him outside, Maggie following behind.

Caught up in Callum's wonder and joy, Nate shoved aside his doubts about Greer and recalled his priorities—being there for Dylan's son if required. Excelling at his job. Deciding that he should take one day at a time with Greer, enjoying whatever time they had together, he gave Callum his full attention, knowing that if Dylan were there, that was exactly what he'd have done.

* * *

Saturday afternoon after a few hours' sleep and an invigorating shower, Greer had felt uplifted as she'd set off in the sunshine to meet Nate at the Seven Dials monument in Covent Garden. Waiting for her when she'd arrived, he'd smiled as if he hadn't seen her for weeks and kissed her as if they were alone before taking her hand in his as they ambled along the cobbled streets of the Seven Dials towards the colourful and trendy Neal's Yard.

'Did you get much sleep?' she asked, because he looked a little tired. As she'd awoken in her own lonely bed two hours ago, there'd been a big part of her that had wished he'd been asleep at her side.

As if she was too far away, he wrapped his arm around her shoulders and drew her close. 'Nah… I promised Callum I'd watch his football match so I went there straight from work this morning.'

'You should have cancelled me,' she said, partly glad that he hadn't. After her silly wobble last night, she was determined to enjoy every last second of their time together. Because she couldn't help but be aware of the ticking clock. They had one week before Lily returned from France. Then Greer would need to focus all her time and energy on Lily's last weeks of living at home. Ensuring she had everything she'd need for uni. Helping her pack. Taking some time off to see Lily settled in Manchester.

'And miss the chance to see you away from work?' Nate said, smiling playfully. 'Are you kidding? If I'd cancelled I wouldn't be able to do this.' He stopped walking, flexed his arm, bringing her lips to his, and kissed her deeply, in the middle of the street. A deliciously decadent kiss she felt all the way down to her flip-flopped toes.

Greer shuddered against him, delicious tendrils of desire snaking along her nerves as she basked in the freedom of touching him whenever she liked.

'You make a good point,' she said when they broke apart, and Nate laughed, pressing his lips to her temple as they ambled on.

'Fancy a gelato?' he asked, pointing out a hole-in-the-wall ice-cream shop with a small queue.

'Always,' she said, laughing, her arm around his waist as they perused the flavours on offer and made their very different selections. A scoop of pistachio topped with another of milk-chocolate pretzel for her and Limoncello and custard cream for Nate.

They sat on a bench in the sun to watch the world go by, his arm around her waist and her hand on his thigh.

'Mm, mine's delicious,' she said, swiping her tongue through the rich creamy flavours, a dreamy state of contentment leaving her relaxed and languid.

'Can I try?' he asked, licking his lips as he watched her eat.

'Sure.' She held up her waffle cone for him to try but he ducked his head, bypassed the ice cream and kissed her lazily, his tongue gliding against hers.

'You're right,' he said when he pulled back and licked his lips the heated look he gave her turning her into a puddle of lust. 'Delicious.'

'Oh, very smooth.' Greer rolled her eyes, secretly delighted that he couldn't seem to keep his hands off her. Because she felt the same way.

They smiled goofily at each other, chat turning to Lily's escapades in Provence and Callum's latest obsession: tadpoles.

'You said you never wanted kids of your own,' Greer said hesitantly, 'but you're clearly a great uncle-figure for Callum. He must adore you.'

Even when their marriage had been good, Mark had rarely attended Lily's extra-curricular activities. He'd always had a surgery, or a private patient to see, or simply relied on Greer making the time because of her shift work.

'I try my best.' He licked a smear of ice cream from his top lip. 'He's so funny. If he could sleep with the tadpoles on his pillow, he would.'

She laughed and leaned her head on his shoulder, his proud smile warming her as effectively as the evening sun.

'He obviously gets that from Dylan,' Nate said quietly. 'He was the same growing up. He loved hard and fast, always flung himself into the obsession of the moment, whether it was a girl at school or his BMX bike or learning the keyboard so he could join a boy band.'

'Was Dylan the oldest?' she asked cautiously, so he didn't shut down again. He obviously wanted to talk about his brother and Greer was intrigued to know how they were similar and different.

'No. I was older by eight minutes.' His sigh was so quiet, she might not have heard it if she'd been sitting any further away.

'What about you and girls and your passions?' she asked. 'Were you similar in that way too?'

Nate shrugged. 'I try to make time for hobbies even though I need to be good at my job. And I'm no slouch when it comes to dating. I've had my fair share of girlfriends.'

Greer chuckled. 'I've no doubt.'

Nate fell silent for moment, then went on. 'But as soon as Dylan met Maggie that was it for him. He'd met the one. That's what makes it harder to accept that he's gone. He had it all, you know. A job he adored, married to the love of his life, a family. He had everything to live for.'

Greer nodded, scared to look up, scared to say

the wrong thing again. 'Is that what you want, too?' she asked, telling herself her interest was selfless. Nate was too young, too sexy and had too much going for him to be alone. She understood why Callum was his priority, but he must one day want similar happiness for himself.

'I've already got the job. As for the love thing…' he said quietly so Greer held her breath, 'maybe one day. But Callum is enough for me when it comes to kids.'

Greer raised her head, a small frown tugging down her brows. 'Don't forget about your own needs and happiness though, will you? I know you have a loyalty to Callum, that you obviously adore each other, but your well-being is just as important as those of the people you love.'

His dedication to his brother's son was admirable. But as a mother, Greer understood how easy it was to prioritise the needs of others above your own. Easy but not always healthy.

His mouth flattened, his stare searching hers. 'You sound like you speak from experience.'

Greer glanced at her lap. 'I guess I do.' She inhaled and met his stare, trying to be more open. 'I've spent the past four years focused on Lily and work, too busy to put myself first, which is easy to justify when you're someone's parent or carer. That doesn't mean it was emotionally healthy.'

'Maybe you were just too nervous to put yourself out there and meet people,' he said softly, his expression devoid of judgement, because she'd already confided as much in him.

'That too.' She nodded, taking a deep inhale. 'Until you came along and asked me on a date, I couldn't really find the energy for worrying about my personal life or meeting someone new. To be honest, thinking about a serious relationship feels terrifying and exhausting, you know? I have enough baggage of my own without taking on someone else's too. And what man in his forties has no baggage?'

Nate nodded thoughtfully, a small smile kicking up his mouth. 'Even us men in our thirties have some. But you do so much for others, Greer. You deserve to think about yourself. You've raised an incredible young woman while being an amazing doctor. And you're too young to just give up on relationships because one went bad.'

Greer looked up, surprised that he saw her so clearly. 'Yes, I am. But I'm not sure I'd bother to ever get married again.'

Nate tilted his head and frowned. 'Even if you were in love?'

'I don't know.' Losing her appetite, Greer tossed what was left of her cone into a nearby bin and wiped her fingers on a napkin. 'With Lily leaving home after the summer, it seems like the perfect time to rediscover myself. To figure out who I am now after divorce and what I want from the rest of my life. To build on the inner strength I had to find when my life crumbled and re-evaluate my boundaries so my next relationship is more…satisfying. On my terms. Know what I mean?'

'I do. And that sounds very healthy,' Nate said, an encouraging smile dancing on his lips. But it quickly faded to be replaced by a frown. 'But maybe you might get remarried, if you met a man you could trust.'

'Maybe.' She ducked her head, the old shame returning, because she'd obviously disappointed him last night. 'I know not all men cheat.' She met his stare. 'And I'm ashamed to say that there was some part of me, even a subconscious part, that went into my marriage almost expecting it to fail because that was my frame of reference.'

Nate nodded sadly. 'Healthy relationships are about mutual respect and good communication. They're always a two-way street. Maybe now that you've been able to analyse some of your past triggers and behaviours, you can go into your next relationship safe and comfortable enough to know you'll be heard.'

Greer nodded, in awe of his emotional intelligence. 'Well, I'm definitely a work in progress,' she laughed, swooping in to steal a kiss because they had veered into some heavy territory. 'Come on.' She stood and pulled him to his feet. 'It's cocktail hour. I'm going to buy you a drink.'

Nate binned his unfinished gelato and slung

his arm over her shoulders once more. 'Can I have beer instead?'

'Of course.' Greer nodded, reaching up to grip his fingers and smiling up at him as they left Neal's Yard and headed towards the Crown and Anchor pub and their delightful beer garden.

CHAPTER THIRTEEN

AFTER THE PUB, where the conversation returned to lighter topics: the football teams they supported—him Arsenal, her Chelsea—the common music they loved, how they each adored everything about Christmas, they headed for the Tube.

Outwardly, Nate smiled and laughed and pulled her close for a kiss whenever the urge arose, which was often, but inside he couldn't help but be unsettled by their conversations these past twenty-four hours. He could understand Greer's trust issues; they made sense given what she'd experienced growing up. But while he craved her trust as much as he craved her kisses, could he expect her to fully trust him when he was hiding something? Or would him telling her his secret only give her another reason to form an unfounded jealousy?

Her reluctance to remarry shouldn't bother him, given this was just casual. But he felt restless, as if, on some level, he needed to prove to her that some men were different. That they could give as much as they took, could communicate effectively, be respectful and considerate and listen.

Inside Covent Garden Underground station, they paused between the eastbound and westbound platforms where they'd need to part. But despite his fatigue and his lingering unease over Greer's ability to handle his revelation if and when he made it, he wasn't ready to say goodbye.

'Come back to my bachelor pad,' he said, smiling roguishly and taking both her hands while his need for her simmered beneath the surface. 'I know Shepherd's Bush isn't Kensington, but I promise I'm fully domesticated. I'm actually a bit of a neat freak and I'm also a whiz in the kitchen. I could make you dinner.'

For a moment she looked as if she might refuse. But then she nodded. 'Okay. I'd love to. If you're sure you're not too tired.'

'Never.' Nate scooped his arm over her shoulders as they alighted the Piccadilly Line train north, exiting one quick stop later at Holborn, before changing to the westbound Central Line. It was standing room only, so Nate held the grab pole with one hand, his other arm around Greer, holding her close so he could enjoy the feel of her body against his as the train carriage rocked.

She clung to his waist to keep her balance against the back-and-forth movement. It was too crowded to have a conversation, the clack of the train on the tracks too loud, but they simply smiled at each other, clearly equally relaxed.

After three stops along their journey, Nate suddenly felt Greer stiffen, her hold on his waist loosen as she glanced down at her feet.

'You okay?' he quietly asked, glancing around the carriage to see a young woman was blatantly staring at them, when everyone knew one of the unspoken Underground rules was to avoid eye contact with fellow passengers.

Greer nodded and looked out of the window at the tunnel walls speeding by. Obviously something had bothered her. As soon as they were outside, he'd ask.

At Shepherd's Bush, they disembarked and climbed the stairs to street level. Near the top of the last flight of stairs, an older woman ahead of them, tightly clutching the hand of a girl who was most likely her granddaughter, slipped and fell onto her knees, crying out in pain and shock.

Greer reached her first, bending to take the woman's elbow. 'Are you okay?'

Nate moved in front and offered her his hand. The woman, who was clearly in some pain, nodded up at them, her embarrassed gaze flicking to her granddaughter.

'I've got arthritis so I can't move quickly.' She reached for the handrail and slowly found one foot on the stair below.

'Just take your time,' Greer said. 'There's no rush.'

But the impatient passengers behind them formed an irritated bottleneck, many offering dirty looks Nate was only too happy to ignore as they streamed around them without offering to help.

'Lean on us,' Nate told the woman as she slowly tried to stand. He positioned his body as a barrier to the flow of passengers rushing to get on with their evenings, shielding the other three from being jostled as best he could.

'Grandma, you're bleeding,' the little girl said, her face pale with worry.

'It's okay. We're doctors,' Nate told them both, glancing at the graze on the woman's knee and the trail of blood dripping down her shin.

'Let's find a member of staff,' Greer said, leading the woman and her granddaughter towards the exit. 'They should have a first-aid kit.'

Finding a customer service assistant, who led them to a chair and produced the first-aid kit, Greer gently cleaned up the woman's knee wound with gauze while Nate tried his best to make the granddaughter smile.

'Doesn't look like it needs stitches,' Nate said, to which Greer nodded in agreement.

'I'll cover it for now,' she said to the woman, 'but when you get home, gently clean it with some disinfectant and replace the dressing.'

‘I’ll be fine,’ the passenger said. ‘Thank you, both. How lucky am I falling in front of two doctors?’ She turned to her granddaughter and added, ‘Silly old Grandma.’

‘It could happen to anyone,’ Nate said as Greer stuck a dressing over the graze. ‘Can I call you a taxi?’ he asked as they exited the station.

‘We only have a short walk, but thank you.’

They watched them leave, then headed in the opposite direction towards Nate’s flat.

‘Some people,’ he said, once more resting his arm on Greer’s shoulders and holding her hand. ‘The dirty looks some of the passengers shot us because they were slowed down for thirty seconds.’

Greer nodded. ‘Yeah. Some people…’ she agreed, but to Nate sounded distracted and tense.

‘You’re kind,’ he said, pressing his lips to her temple.

‘So are you.’ She smiled up at him.

‘Wc make a good team, then,’ he said as they crossed the road and headed for his flat.

Nate’s ‘bachelor pad’ turned out to be a bright and stylish two-bedroom apartment on the top floor of a charming Edwardian red-brick mansion overlooking Spencer Green, a leafy urban park popular with families, dog walkers and joggers. The large sun-drenched reception room gave way to an open-plan dining room and kitchen where

Nate was clearly very much at home. Sexily so, although Greer was obviously biased.

'Red wine or white?' he asked, retrieving two glasses from a sleek-fronted modern wall cabinet.

'Red, please,' she answered, taking a seat at the island to watch him pour the wine while she tried to brush off what had happened on the Tube.

She'd been having a lovely evening, enjoying the sunshine and bustle of the city. Enjoying Nate's uplifting company and frequent touches. Holding hands, his arm around her shoulders, the way he seemed as addicted to their kisses as she was. Then she'd looked up and caught someone staring at them on the train and all her doubts had resurfaced like repeated blows from a heavyweight boxer.

'Is pasta okay for dinner?' he asked, filling a pan with water, adding a pinch of coarse sea salt and placing it on the ceramic hob.

'Great,' Greer said, although she wasn't particularly hungry. Nate was observing her cautiously as if he knew her fears and doubts. As if she were made of glass. She didn't want to hurt him or make him feel as if she didn't want to be there, so she smiled brightly as he turned from the stove.

'To summer dates and gelato,' Nate said, touching his glass to hers.

'Cheers.' She held his eye contact as they each sipped.

Nate reached for her hand and led her to a comfy sofa, where she kicked off her flip-flops and leaned into his side, her head resting on his chest. He'd put some music on when they'd arrived and she listened for a few moments, trying to rediscover the contentment she'd felt earlier.

'What happened on the Tube?' he asked after another moment's silence, his heart thudding under her cheek. 'I noticed you became uncomfortable suddenly.'

Greer swallowed, wishing she could hide the truth or dismiss his concern, but she respected him too much to even try, especially after how she'd behaved last night.

'Just a silly moment. *My* silly moment,' she said, looking up and brushing his lips with hers. 'Someone was staring at us and it suddenly hit home why. That it was most likely because I'm older than you. I'd kind of mostly forgotten that this past week, believe it or not.' But the staring woman on the train was just another reminder that, as great as he was, Nate wasn't the man for her.

Nate slid his thumb over her knuckles. 'I *can* believe it, Greer. When I look at you, when I'm with you, I'm not thinking about the numbers and the arbitrary norms acceptable by society. I'm just in the moment with you, a woman I enjoy spending time with, can laugh with and who I also find as sexy as sin.'

Greer chuckled softly. She felt exactly the same about him. Then she fell serious. 'I haven't been thinking about our age gap this whole time either. I guess her staring today made me question it again. We're at different life stages, you and I. I've been married and you have that to come. You have time to test out relationships until you find the one. Whereas I don't have the luxury of making another big mistake. I almost have an adult daughter and—'

'I have Callum,' he interrupted, clearly uncomfortable with her comparisons.

'Yes.' She nodded again, lowering her stare from his. 'I guess, up until today, I've convinced myself that our handful of stolen moments during the night shift, our conversations, our first kiss, even that incredibly hot sex we had in the on-call room… It's all felt like a dream. A very sexy, forbidden dream that makes me want to stay asleep a bit longer.'

'I get that,' he said, a thoughtful frown pinching his brows together.

And yet for all her maturity in years, sometimes, like now, he made her feel inexperienced somehow, vulnerable and afraid of the power of their connection. When they were alone, when she was caught up in him, the rest of the world, her worries and hang-ups just disappeared. But they were there beneath the surface. And they were real.

'Come here.' Patting his lap, he urged her to sit astride his thighs. He cupped her face, his stare locked to hers. 'This is just about us. You and me. No one else matters.'

'I know.' Greer nodded, awash with embarrassment that she'd allowed such an irrelevance as the judgement of a stranger to get into her head. 'How is it that sometimes you seem like the mature one?' Open and communicative and dauntless.

He smiled sadly, as if he'd expected her to be over this issue by now. 'We don't just make a good team,' he went on, 'we're also good together, aren't we? Is it just me who feels it? Because from where I'm standing, what we have is pretty special.'

She nodded again. 'I feel it too.' But just because they were a great team at work and clicked in the bedroom, shared a sense of humour and were comfortable with each other, didn't change the facts.

Nate was in his prime. He deserved all the things Dylan had had. And Greer wasn't sure she was ready to look for love again.

'Our private life is just that, Greer: private. We don't owe anyone an explanation or justification. We don't have to apologise or make ourselves smaller to make strangers feel comfortable in their narrow beliefs or opinions.'

'You're right.' She nodded once more, her

breathing tight because he seemed to see and understand her so clearly.

'And aside from the fact that we're not engaged,' he went on, 'that this is a fling, what's the difference between you and me and your ex and his fiancée?'

'Nothing,' she agreed. 'I don't want to feel this way… I just…' She faltered, scared that her unhelpful thinking might simply be her fear at play. Because when she was with Nate, it sometimes felt so right she had to catch herself and remember that it wasn't a serious relationship. That it couldn't go anywhere. That it would soon be over.

'Maybe it's because the patriarchy runs the world,' he said, his expression sardonic. 'It's okay for a man to date a woman half his age, but not the other way around.' He smiled sadly as if taking the responsibility of every man on his shoulders, and Greer smiled back, loving that he cared so passionately.

'I mean, it's not really okay,' she said, feeling lighter for having shared her thoughts with him. 'If Lily brought home a forty-year-old boyfriend I'd have a lot to say about it, but I appreciate your point. Thanks for talking me down from the ledge. I guess I've just been so engrossed in this sexy guy I'm seeing, a part of me isn't ready for the bubble to burst.'

Nate searched her stare, his turning serious.

'Why does it have to burst? Can't we keep it intact a while longer and see how it goes?'

'Yes.' Greer nodded, her heart thudding because part of her wanted exactly that. 'I'm sorry I freaked out. Again. I told you it was silly.'

Nate shook his head. 'Nothing you feel is silly.'

Sighing, she leaned down and pressed her lips to his, sliding her fingers into his hair, tilting his head back as she touched her tongue to his, kissing him freely and deeply, exploring him until his hands fisted gently in her hair and he groaned. Desire for him bloomed anew, crushing all other feelings until she forgot about the world outside, forgot her responsibilities. She even forgot to play it cool and simply lived in the moment with Nate.

'Turn off the pasta water,' she said, when, panting, they broke apart.

Nate stared up at her with desire-darkened eyes and nodded. 'Hold on,' he said, cupping her backside and standing, carrying her to the kitchen, where she reached down and turned off the hob, before he strode to his bedroom and lowered her to the bed.

They stripped in silence, their stares hungrily roaming each other's naked bodies, their constant need for each other clearly matched. When they lay face to face, their palms gliding over skin, their legs entwined as they kissed and kissed, Greer closed her eyes, basking in the perfect moment of connection with this incredible man. A man who'd given her back a part of herself she hadn't realised was missing.

Nate cupped her cheeks, stroking her hair back from her face as he pressed kisses over her closed eyelids. 'I see you, Greer. I know you've been hurt before. I know you've struggled with trust because of your parents and your past. But I'm not the kind of man to cheat or mess around.'

Greer opened her eyes and swallowed at the honest vulnerability she saw in his. 'I know,' she whispered, wishing she could feel this certainty for ever.

'If I wanted anyone else, I wouldn't be here with you,' Nate said, staring deep into her eyes.

Greer nodded, emotion welling in her throat as she held him close. 'I want you too, Nate. I don't think anyone has ever seen me as clearly as you do. It's…scary.'

Because he'd shattered every assumption she'd made about him. Showing her over and over again his emotional depth and complexities. His incredible strength and empathy. His maturity and dependability.

He nodded, sighing. 'I know. I… I feel it too. I… I want you all the time.'

'I'm right here.' Determined to look no further ahead than today, Greer slid her fingers into his hair and brought his mouth back to hers. His kisses, deep and drugging, silenced her doubts.

His fiercely possessive touch soothed her fears. In his arms, free to be herself, anything seemed possible and she knew exactly who she was. Knew that he wouldn't hurt her just as she wouldn't hurt him.

'Nate,' she moaned as he captured her nipple with his mouth, sucking as he stroked between her legs, drowning out everything but the clamour of sensation and need.

Reaching for the condom he'd tossed on the bed earlier, she covered him and pulled him on top of her, parting her thighs to accommodate his hips, kissing him again as he slid his fingers between hers and pressed their joined hands into the mattress.

'Do you trust me?' he asked, peering down at her, his eyes determined and dark with desire.

'Yes.' Greer nodded, her lips chasing his once more as he pushed inside her and she groaned, crossing her ankles in the small of his back.

'Look at me,' he demanded, his hips beginning to move so all she could do was cling to him and ride out the surges of pleasure and obey. She gasped at the dark possessive look on his face.

'This is about us, Greer,' he said, his expression fierce. 'Just us.'

She nodded, too turned on to speak, too lost to do anything but grip his hands and stare back as he drove them both higher and higher, his thrusts faster and harder.

'Nate,' she gasped, her orgasm all but tearing her apart as he groaned, reared up and, with a final jerk, his face twisted in blissful release, came too.

CHAPTER FOURTEEN

'WHY DON'T YOU stay the night?' Nate asked sleepily as Greer hunted the bedroom floor for her underwear. The twenty-four hours without sleep was finally catching up with him. His eyelids felt made of lead. He couldn't even muster the strength to properly admire naked Greer, who was gorgeously dishevelled, her skin still flushed from her orgasm. He wanted to shower with her, wash every inch of her body and then fall asleep with her in his arms, waking her up with morning sex until she was too pleasure-drunk to overthink what was happening between them, too consumed by this to care about other people and had to rely solely on feelings. Because when they were together, he too forgot his doubts and fears.

'I can't. I have a ton of things to do tomorrow, including cleaning the flat. Lily is home Saturday. It's her birthday. I'm throwing her a surprise eighteenth party.'

'Okay.' Nate rose too and pulled on his boxers, certain from the hollowness in the middle of his chest that his addiction to Greer had reached new heights and that he already had feelings for her. The idea of simply walking away from this the minute her daughter returned from France made him want to throw up. But Greer, despite her assurances that she trusted him, despite their growing connection, hadn't mentioned revising the plan.

'Next Saturday…' he mumbled, knowing that if he weren't so tired he'd seize this moment to discover Greer's thoughts. 'That's come around pretty quickly.'

Every bone in his body ached with resistance at the arbitrary cut-off she'd set. But since when had he been passive? If he wanted something, he went after it, fatigued or not.

Greer pulled on her jeans and looked up with uncertainty and a flash of guilt. 'I… I wondered if you'd like to come to the party,' she said with only a hint of hesitancy. 'I've invited my ex and his fiancée, Cara. She's asked Lily to be her bridesmaid and if she's going to be my daughter's stepmother, I'd like to know her better. And some of the ED nurses too. The ones who've met Lily over the years.'

Nate picked up her T-shirt and held it out to her, his heart leaping with excitement even as he told himself to calm down. 'I'd love to come, if you want me there.'

It was a small step but maybe it meant she was

ready for them to step out of the shadows. To stop all the secrets and sneaking around. To have a shot at making this fling a real relationship.

'Of course,' Greer said, pulling the shirt on, 'it's just a barbecue with Lily's school friends and plus ones mainly. Very casual.'

Because she was distracted and acting flustered, as if already stressing about the event, Nate snaked an arm around her waist, pulled her body flush to his and kissed her, slowly, lazily, deeply. She sighed, crossing her arms over his shoulders, pressing his head closer with her forearms so the kiss deepened and she moaned.

Holding her waist, he pulled back. 'I know we agreed to stop seeing each other when Lily returns, but I don't want this to be our last week together.' His pulse buzzed in his ears as he held his breath.

'I know.' She winced, her eyes darting away. 'I just… We need to be careful. I don't want Lily to be confused or hurt by this. Us. I don't want to act like Mark, forcing her to meet all his casual conquests as if it legitimised the relationships that obviously weren't destined to last. I haven't even told her that I'm dating someone. I need to tread carefully, because she'll be gone again in a matter of weeks to Manchester.'

Nate nodded in understanding, relieved that they were on the same page, that neither of them was ready for this to end, even as unease tensed his shoulders at the idea of Greer dating a string of men after him. 'You'll tell her in your own time. Don't put any pressure on yourself. Just know that I'm here if you need me. For anything. Minor freak-outs. Dinner I promise to finish next time. Mature advice dressed in cartoon socks.'

Nate understood this relationship was difficult for her. In addition to her previous trust issues, she feared judgement over their age gap and professional embarrassment because he was her registrar. But if they wanted to make this work, he knew she'd work through all of that in time. And he'd give her that time. After all, she was worth waiting for.

'Thanks.' She looked up and smiled with shining eyes. 'I'm going to go,' she said, pressing her mouth to his in a restrained kiss. 'You need to sleep before you collapse.'

'Can I see you after work, Monday?' he asked. 'Before you start the night shift?'

She smiled and nodded. 'Absolutely. Just come round to Willow Gardens when you finish. We've barely made a dent in that jumbo box of condoms.'

'Challenge accepted.' Nate grinned and shot her a flirty wink. 'It's a date.'

At the door to his flat, she pressed her lips to his one final time, her hand cupping his bristled cheek. 'Sleep well.'

And then she was gone, taking a small slice

of his peace of mind with her, because no matter what they'd said to reassure each other, no matter how strongly his feelings were when they were together, once apart Nate too felt the pressure of his doubts.

His secret grew heavier. He didn't want to let Greer down. He didn't want to fall for another woman who might not tolerate his relationship with Dylan's family. But stronger than either of those was his fear of once more failing someone he loved. And when it came to Greer, to the feelings he was desperately trying to untangle, he might already be headed in that direction.

By Friday, a new work-life pattern had developed, one for which Nate could develop a serious addiction. He'd finish his day shift at the hospital and race straight around to Greer's place. They'd spend an hour in bed, the sex intense and desperate because of the time restraints and the fact that their freedom to see each other as much as they wanted would end once Lily arrived home. Then they'd shower together and walk hand in hand to the Tube station, where they'd part, Greer headed for the hospital and her night shift and Nate headed home to crash.

Energised to repeat the pattern and see Greer later that evening, Nate arrived early for his day shift and got straight to work. His first patient of the day was a thirty-nine-year-old man with chest pain and shortness of breath. As the nurses wheeled the patient into Resus, adjusting the oxygen flow through his mask and attaching him to the cardiac monitors, Nate quickly spoke to the paramedic for some history.

'He's an oncology patient here,' the paramedic said. 'Had an orchidectomy for testicular cancer eight weeks ago. Had his third round of chemotherapy last week. He's tachycardic, respiratory rate of twenty-two and his blood pressure is low.'

Nate listened, while he began his observations of the patient, noting the man's blue lips, a sign of central cyanosis, and corresponding low oxygen saturations.

'Hi, Matt, I'm Nate, one of the emergency doctors here. I need to examine you and run some tests.'

He fitted his stethoscope and listened to the patient's heart, noting that his ECG appeared normal apart from sinus tachycardia. Some chemotherapy agents could be cardiotoxic, causing heart failure or arrhythmias.

'Do we have the notes?' Nate asked Harry. 'Check the chemotherapy agents he's received and call his oncologist and Radiology. We need an urgent chest X-ray.'

Needing to exclude pneumonia or a pulmonary embolism, Nate listened to the patient's breath sounds, closing his eyes to focus amid the noises of the room: shoes squeaking on the linoleum, the beep of monitors, the whoosh of the door swinging open and shut. Nate could hear crackles at the lung bases when he listened, telling him the lungs were waterlogged because the heart was under strain, but there was another sound too. A subtle creaking on auscultation of the chest, a sign called a pleural rub, an indication of an infarcted lung grating on the pleura.

'Is Dr Thorn still here?' Nate asked Sally, one of the nurses, when he'd completed his examination. His suspected diagnosis was a pulmonary embolism. He felt confident he was right, but it wouldn't hurt to have a second opinion, especially in a case like this that was complicated by a recent cancer diagnosis and chemotherapy.

'She's with a stroke patient next door,' Sally said, apologetically, and Nate nodded. 'I haven't seen Dr Huxtable yet this morning,' Sally said about the consultant on the day shift today. 'Do you want me to page him?'

Nate nodded. 'Thanks, Sally. But first let's start an anticoagulant infusion.' Nate reached for a syringe to take an arterial sample from the man's wrist to measure his arterial blood gas levels.

Just then the radiologist arrived and, using the portable X-ray machine, quickly took a chest X-ray.

'Order an urgent V/Q scan,' Nate told Harry, who rushed to the computer to do just that. The ventilation-perfusion scan would definitively identify a pulmonary embolism.

While everyone present rushed to treat the life-threatening condition, the worst happened. The patient slumped and fell unconscious. The cardiac monitor alarms sounded, and when Nate tried to find a pulse, there wasn't one.

'Call the crash team,' he said, reaching for an oropharyngeal airway and a manual resuscitation bag. 'Start CPR.'

Sally began chest compressions. Nate glanced at the cardiac monitor. The patient's heart was in asystole or flat-line. Just then, the crash team arrived, the anaesthetist taking over the patient's breathing so Nate could administer the adrenaline.

Greer too arrived, looking tired as she glanced at Nate for an explanation.

'Suspected massive pulmonary embolism,' he told her, flushing the adrenaline that might restart the man's heart into his IV. 'He's a post-op chemotherapy patient, stage two testicular cancer.'

Greer nodded, her expression grim but determined as she took over chest compressions from the nurse, while Nate kept time, monitored the heart's rhythm and administered more adrenaline.

After ten minutes, the heart rhythm was unchanged, the prognosis poor. At some stage the patient's oncologist had arrived, the woman warily watching the resuscitation attempts from the sidelines. Nate looked to her now for her guidance.

She pressed her lips together, her expression similar to every other person's in the room. Resignation tempered by a glimmer of hope. It seemed no one was ready to make the call to stop CPR, least of all Nate. But it was his job to make such calls. Yes, the outlook for this patient was poor given the diagnosis and the prolonged period of resuscitation. The potential for the patient's recovery without permanent neurological consequences was dwindling as time went on. But Nate refused to give up on someone so young. Someone not much older than him, someone like Dylan.

'Is everyone happy to keep going?' Nate asked, making the judgement call and his position clear.

Everyone nodded, Greer included.

'Get me a central line kit,' Nate told Sally, quickly washing up and pulling on sterile gloves. 'I need an rtPA infusion.'

Administered directly into a major vein, the clot-dissolving drug might be enough to treat the embolus in the man's lung and allow his heart to function once more. It was certainly worth a shot with other options dwindling.

Standing beside the anaesthetist who'd intubated the patient, Nate inserted the catheter into the man's jugular vein and attached the infusion.

With his last-ditch attempt complete, Nate looked up to find Greer staring at him with sympathy. She knew him, knew what he was thinking: that if there was any chance of recovery, Nate would do what he could. And she also knew why he was fighting so hard, because he'd confided in her about Dylan and his regrets. But he couldn't be distracted by that now.

The CPR continued for another fifteen minutes, during which Nate became increasingly despondent. Then, suddenly, just as he thought he might have to re-evaluate the decision to keep going, the heart rhythm changed and everyone immediately felt for a pulse.

'I've got one,' Greer said, looking to Nate with relief.

'Me too.' He kept his fingers on the man's carotid artery, never more relieved to feel the rhythmic beat of life against his fingertips.

'Call ICU,' Nate instructed Harry as some members of the crash team departed, their roles over now that the patient had been resuscitated. 'And chase the chest X-ray results.'

Sally, next to him, touched his arm and said quietly, 'Well done, Dr Hunter.'

Nate nodded, relieved that his efforts to resuscitate the patient had succeeded. He looked around for Greer, but she'd already left too, replaced by Dr Huxtable. The consultant on the day shift.

It was only hours after the emergency that Nate realised that Greer would normally have offered him a secret look or word of approval after they'd worked on a case together. It shouldn't bother him. He could do his job without her support. They were busy medical professionals for whom the job, the patient, always came first. And she would be at home asleep by now after her night shift.

But as he went about his work day with Greer constantly at the back of his mind, Nate realised how deeply he was in this. He ached, constantly craving her, addicted to her smile, her support and whatever scraps of her time he could get. Fearful that, despite what she said, she didn't fully trust him. Certainly his feelings seemed to eclipse hers, and if he wasn't careful, if he laid himself bare, told Greer his secret shame and opened himself up entirely to her and she didn't feel the same way, he'd be devastated.

With only her message on his phone to tide him over—meet you at Spencer Green after your shift—Nate shoved away the thought that maybe the time had come to tell Greer about Maggie and focused on work.

CHAPTER FIFTEEN

LATER THAT DAY, Greer awoke to find a message from Nate saying he'd be home at 4:00 p.m. Unsettled by what she'd witnessed earlier at the hospital—Nate's heavy emotional investment in his patient—Greer packed her work bag and headed over to his place on the Tube.

She pressed the buzzer to his apartment, her stomach knotted with apprehension. She understood how easy it was to be affected by some cases. Doctors were only human. For Nate, this morning's cardiac arrest patient had most likely reminded him a little too closely of his brother. But for Greer it had been a sign that, while he took pride in being good at his job, there were clearly underlying emotions that drove Nate, who maybe wasn't as far along in the grieving process as she'd assumed. Her need to make sure he was okay even eclipsed the niggle of lingering jealousy she'd experienced when nurse Sally had touched him after the arrest.

'Come up,' Nate said through the intercom,

the buzzer sounding and the front door lock disabling with a metallic click. When she reached his floor, Nate stood in the open doorway of his apartment, looking tired, his stare a little wary.

'Hi,' she said, sliding her arm around his waist as she pressed her lips to his. 'How are you doing?'

'I'm fine,' he said, leading her into the kitchen, where she placed her bag on a bar stool. 'Do you want a cold drink?'

She nodded and he fixed them each a tall glass of tonic water with ice and a slice of lemon.

'Shame there's no gin in it,' she said, trying to be playful then taking a sip to calm her nerves.

He gave her a small smile then watched her carefully, his expression guarded. Maybe he was expecting another jealous cold shoulder.

'I'm sorry about this morning,' she began. 'Sally came looking for me saying you needed help, but by the time I got there the arrest was in full swing. Any idea how the patient is doing?' Because there was too much distance between them, she abandoned her drink and stepped close, wrapping her arms around his waist and resting her head over the reassuring thud of his heart.

'He's still unconscious in ICU,' he said flatly, his arm around her shoulders and his chin resting on the top of her head as he held her close.

'You did everything you could, Nate. Now it's just a waiting game to gauge his recovery.'

Nate nodded, the tension in his body palpable so she could tell he was in no way convinced.

'I'm really sorry I wasn't there for you when you needed me,' she said softly. 'After the arrest, I had no legitimate reason to hang around the emergency department on the off chance we'd have a moment to speak. You were busy. I didn't want to arouse suspicion by waiting for you.'

'It's okay,' he said. 'I understand, Greer. Although right now, I'm struggling to care about suspicions that we might be more than colleagues. But I understand you feel a degree of professional responsibility, given our positions.'

'Of course I do.' Greer blinked, shocked by his candour, feeling uncertain of him in this mood. 'I'm not sure I'm ready to simply announce us to the world.' In fact as the days passed, as Lily's return approached, she was less and less sure of everything beyond the fact that she couldn't seem to control her physical addiction to Nate.

'Don't worry.' He scrubbed a hand over his face. 'I'm just tired. It's been a long day.'

Greer winced, watching him closely. She cared about him the way he cared about her. She couldn't simply stand by and see him struggle with his guilt over Dylan.

'Listen, I know it's hard to be objective sometimes,' she continued, stepping back to face him, 'especially when patients are young. When they remind us of someone we know or we can put ourselves in their shoes or those of their loved ones. I've been there, too.'

When he stayed silent, watching her with an expression more haunted than when she'd first arrived, Greer pressed her lips together. She seemed to be making things worse, not better. He clearly didn't want to talk about this.

Suddenly, as if coming to a decision, Nate stepped forwards and reached for her, kissing her hard and fast and desperately as if he'd waited too long or wanted to halt further conversation. Aching for him and the demons he was so clearly still struggling with, Greer kissed him back, her hands sliding under his shirt, her tongue sliding against his as she became engulfed in familiar desires.

'I missed you,' he said desperately, his lips gliding along her jaw, his fingers sliding into her hair. 'I know it's crazy because we see each other all the time. But… I don't want this to be over.'

'Nate,' Greer moaned as his hand slid along her thigh under her skirt. 'I missed you too. It's not over.' Not yet, although maybe Nate could hear the same ticking clock she could hear. And as much as she was trying to trust him, her demons weren't silent either.

He pressed her back against the counter, hoisting her up onto the edge and standing between her spread thighs to deepen their kiss and then pull back.

'I need you,' he said, their eyes locked as his fingers delved inside her underwear, stroking and teasing and sending spirals of delicious pleasure along her legs down to her toes.

'I need you too.' She pulled at his T-shirt and he tossed it away. Then she reached for his fly, popping the button of his jeans and shoving them and his boxers over his hips to free his erection.

'Condom in my bag,' she mumbled as he kissed her again. While she reached for the bag, Nate peeled her underwear down, his hand back between her legs, his fingers sliding inside her so she gasped.

'Hurry,' she said, handing him the condom, desperate now to reaffirm their connection to banish the emotional day and silence all the noisy doubts.

While he put it on she kissed his face, his neck, his shoulders and chest, sliding her tongue over his skin, breathing in the comforting scent of him to hold it like a memory. He was such an incredible man. She could hold onto this, take one day at a time. Show him she did trust him.

She gripped his shoulders. He wrapped one arm around her hips and held her in place, pushed inside her, while they kissed and moaned.

'Yes, Nate,' she said, clinging to him as they moved, fast and frantic. She wrapped her thighs around his waist and he held them in his hands, chasing her mouth as if he couldn't bear for one part of them to be separated.

They came together, her with a blissful cry and him with an agonised groan he uttered against the side of her neck as his breaths heaved and his arms tightened, holding her close.

As they caught their breath, Greer stroked his back, surprised by his tight grip on her. Something subtle had changed between them. Nate seemed withdrawn, as if, despite what he'd said about wanting more time, this was coming to its natural end. Or maybe he recognised both her lingering trust issues and her growing doubts, saw how conflicted she was, desperate for him one minute, hardening her heart the next because it surely had to end some time. And she didn't want either of them to be hurt.

'Are you okay?' she whispered, remembering what he'd been through and why, for him, today might have been a tough one.

He nodded, looked up and slowly withdrew, helping her down from the counter. 'I'll be back in a second. Don't go anywhere. I need to talk to you.'

While he was in the bathroom, Greer pulled on her underwear and ran her fingers through her hair, her stomach hollow with the idea she was responsible for their situation. Yes, Nate had asked her out on a date. But she could have shut him down. Made it clear that she wouldn't tolerate such a lapse in professional judgement on her part. But it was too late now. She'd been flattered and weak. She'd allowed herself to know him, to see him as clearly as he saw her. And now she wanted him to be happy and fulfilled regardless of how long this relationship could last.

'I want to talk to you, too,' she said when he came back from the bathroom.

He reached for her hand and led her to the sofa, where he pulled her down to sit at his side.

'You go first,' he said, a frown pinching his brows together.

She squeezed his fingers, his strange mood and her guilt for her possessive thoughts over Sally leaving her uncertain where to begin. She didn't want to overstep again and make him withdraw, but after today nor could she stay silent. 'I wanted you to know that, just like you see me, I also see you,' she said softly. She could sense he was holding back. Throwing all he had into his job and Callum when he had so much more to give for the right woman.

'It struck me this morning after the cardiac arrest,' she said, 'that the reason you were maybe not as objective as at other times is because of Dylan.'

He frowned deeper and Greer rushed on. 'I think you're struggling to forgive yourself for not spotting that Dylan was sick. Maybe you're even telling yourself that you don't deserve to be happy because you let him down or because he's not here to feel the same way. But that's not true, Nate. You do deserve that. You—'

He began to shake his head, dismissing her observations before she'd even finished.

She gripped both his hands, urging him to hear what she had to say. 'What happened to Dylan wasn't your fault. Just because we're doctors, doesn't mean we're not also human. It doesn't mean we can fix everyone. And I'm sure Dylan wouldn't want you to feel guilty or hold yourself responsible. He loved you like you love him. He'd want you to be happy, too. You have to let this guilt go and forgive yourself so you can be fulfilled. So you can have the things Dylan had and loved, if you want them.'

She wasn't sure how long they could continue this relationship, how long it would meet both their needs, but, like Nate, part of her wasn't ready to walk away. If she could help him see that his guilt wasn't healthy, maybe she'd have no regrets when it did end.

'I know I can't fix everyone,' he said, his voice strained. 'And I appreciate your concern. But—' He broke off and exhaled loudly, looking away. Wordlessly, he got to his feet and paced over to the window, turned and paced back, coming to stand still before Greer.

'You're right. I do feel guilty,' he said, a frustrated edge to his voice. 'I always will. Blaming myself for missing my brother's diagnosis isn't rational, I know. But I've felt responsible for him my whole life. I let him down. I was the eldest. Those eight minutes mattered to me and part of me is terrified to forget Dylan. But there's something else, Greer. The thing I want to tell you. Something I'm not proud of. Something I wish I could undo but can't.'

'It's okay. Whatever it is. You can forgive yourself for that, too.'

He shook his head, scrubbed a hand over his face then met her stare, his almost pleading. 'I… really like you, Greer. I'd like to keep seeing you. I think we could have a real relationship, but I have to tell you this first.'

'So tell me.' Dread knotted in the pit of her stomach. 'Is it to do with Sally? I noticed how close you two were this morning.'

'What? No.' Nate scowled, confused and obviously hurt by her assumption. 'It's nothing to do with anyone but me. I… Can you just listen for a moment?'

'Okay.' Her heart was beating so fast she wondered if she might be sick.

Nate retook his seat and reached for both her hands. 'After Dylan died, I was a mess.'

She nodded, her heart sore. Of course he would have been a mess. She wouldn't expect anything else.

'I kept waiting for it to get easier the way they

say—that rubbish about time healing. But it didn't work. Every morning I'd wake up struck with the same sickening shock that I'd awoken to a world where he no longer existed. The only thing that helped me back then was Callum. I had to be strong for him. If he wanted to cry, I had to simply sit with him, hold him. If he had questions about his dad, I tried to answer them as honestly as I could. Maggie was in a state too. I began spending so much time at their place, Callum would ask me for a bedtime story, because that had been his and Dylan's thing.'

Greer nodded, her eyes stinging for their loss.

'Then one night, months after the funeral, Maggie and I were talking about Dylan and crying after Callum was asleep as we often did over a glass of Dylan's favourite beer, and out of nowhere we were kissing.'

Greer froze, the swallow she took painful as she tried to keep her expression neutral.

'I know,' he said, his jaw clenched. 'One thing led to another and we slept together. I hated myself immediately after, and so did Maggie. We instantly regretted it, cried some more and each swore that would never happen again. But even if I'd wanted to put some space between us, I couldn't abandon Callum, not when I'd somehow partially filled this void Dylan had left behind.'

'That was why your ex got jealous,' she said, the pieces slotting into place. 'Why she couldn't tolerate your close relationship with Maggie. You told her, didn't you?'

Hot spikes of jealousy she wished she didn't feel stabbed at her chest. Nate and Maggie were still close.

Nate nodded. 'And why I've wanted to tell you, wanted to explain why my grief and my guilt is so…complex. Why I push myself to be good at my job so me letting my brother down isn't in vain. I messed up, Greer. I let Dylan down twice. Once when he was sick and then again by acting out and trying to numb the pain of his death. I was his older brother. It was my job to never let him down.'

Greer nodded, numbly. 'You could have told me sooner, although I understand why you kept it from me.' She winced, hearing the unfair accusation in her words.

Nate frowned. 'I didn't *keep it* from you. I didn't want it to be an issue between us but nor did I know where this relationship was going.'

Greer nodded, unable to sift through the mix of her feelings as a sickening sense of déjà vu clouded her thoughts, transporting her back in time to a hundred other moments when she'd struggled to trust and doubted her instincts.

'Part of me didn't want you to judge me,' Nate went on. 'My ex tried to make me choose between her and Dylan's family.'

'That wasn't fair of her,' Greer said, realising how close she'd come to judging him too because of her issues. 'You made an error of judgement before you met her. It was unreasonable for her to expect you to cut ties with your family, especially when you and Maggie were over.' But despite her seeing his ex's behaviour rationally, there was still a part of Greer that could relate to the jealousy element.

'Me and Maggie were never a thing,' he said, firmly. 'It was a grief-stricken moment of madness. An unhealthy coping mechanism like binge drinking.'

'I know…' Greer nodded in understanding even as her stomach rolled again at the idea of Nate and Maggie's relationship, those old demons of hers close to the surface. Nate wasn't her father, wasn't Mark, but she couldn't help the shudder of doubt that skittered over her skin like a shiver. She'd opened up to this man, been vulnerable with him, despite her former misgivings for beginning a romantic relationship. It was only natural to feel unsettled by his revelation, especially when he'd kept it a secret all these weeks.

'I was scared that if you knew it might push you away,' Nate said, cupping her face and pressing a swift kiss to her lips, his expression hopeful and relieved. 'But I no longer wanted to keep it a secret from you. I even told Maggie about you. She's excited to meet you.'

'You told Maggie about me?' Greer's stomach tightened, sickeningly. If Nate had confided in Maggie about their fling, the two of them obviously had a *very* close relationship. And if it was definitely over between him and Maggie, if there was no longer anything to tell, if it was all harmless, why keep it a secret at all?

'Yes, because I care about you, Greer. I was excited and told her I had a date. But I haven't told her your name or any specifics. I wouldn't do that.'

'I know.' Greer nodded, ignoring his declaration. She had feelings for him too, but it was clearly time for a reality check. Would she feel that old familiar wavering of trust if she was ready for a real serious relationship? Over Sally's innocent pat on the arm and now the idea of Nate and Maggie? Clearly her recent misgivings and doubts about taking this beyond a secret fling were justified. Warnings she should perhaps heed before she got hurt again. Before this went any further and became another mistake.

Aware that Nate was waiting for a response, Greer swallowed past her dry throat. Her chest tightened, her stomach swirling. She needed space. Air. She needed to get away from him so she could think clearly. So she could untangle how she truly felt. Because maybe Nate was right. Maybe she couldn't fully trust him.

Greer's discomfort was obvious in the set of her mouth and her lowered gaze as she stood up. Nate's fingers curled into a fist and he released a frustrated sigh as he felt her slipping away. 'Do you know that about me?' he asked, frowning. She'd said she trusted him and now she was looking at him as if he were a stranger.

'Yes, of course…'

The lack of conviction in her voice sent his mind spiralling. 'You've heard every word I've said? Because I know you've struggled with trust in the past, but me and Maggie… It's not like that. Nor is there anything going on with me and Sally, for that matter. Tell me you understand that, Greer? I thought you trusted me.'

He couldn't hide his hurt and frustration. He'd assumed they'd moved past bouts of unfounded jealousy, but maybe Greer wasn't as invested in him as he was in her. Maybe he was falling for another woman who might not support his relationship with Dylan's family.

'I do understand,' she said. 'I've heard everything you said. Thanks for telling me about Maggie. I… I'm sorry I can't stay longer.' She stood, her gaze flicking towards the door. 'I need to go. I said I'd start an hour early tonight to cover for Dr Jameson.'

She sounded fatigued and resigned. Distant.

'Wait.' Panicked, Nate reached for her hand and stood too, confused that he'd poured out his heart and Greer was simply leaving, although he understood that she needed to work. 'You look like you don't believe me. You're acting like it's an issue for you.'

Greer shook her head. 'No. I do believe you. I just… I'm surprised, that's all. I wasn't expecting that revelation. I understand how grief affects people in many ways. What you've told me doesn't make me think any less of you, Nate.' She placed her hand on top of his, giving him hope. 'I hate to rush off but I have to go to work. I can't really think about this right now. Can I call you tomorrow?'

Nate pressed his lips together in frustration. 'Of course.'

Greer nodded and headed for the kitchen to collect her bag. 'I'll call you when I get home from the hospital tomorrow morning.' She walked to the door, as if desperate to get away.

Nate followed her, leaned in to press his lips to hers in a kiss that felt pleading and frantic. Irritation and panic swirled in Nate in equal measure. It felt as if he were losing her when he'd not only made himself vulnerable but had also hoped they were past mistrust.

Before she could leave, he asked, 'Do you… do you still want me at the party?' He held his breath anticipating her answer, which might go either way.

'Of course,' she said, and Nate winced at the wobble of uncertainty in her voice.

'And if I do come,' he pushed, hating their polite distance, 'how will you describe me to people? A work colleague?'

'I… I hadn't really thought. But yes…' She flushed and glanced down. 'I guess a friend is the safest option.' She looked up, her stare vulnerable and so full of fear Nate felt sick. 'You've met Lily before. And some of the ED nurses will be there.'

Nate nodded, biting back his feelings and the things he wanted to say.

As if she sensed his turmoil, she raised her chin, her stare hardening. 'Tomorrow is all about Lily, Nate. I don't want to make it about me or us. I hope you understand.'

'Of course I do,' he said, hurt that she felt the need to remind him of her priorities and his place in them.

She stepped close and pressed a kiss to his cheek. 'See you tomorrow.'

Then she was gone without a backward glance, leaving Nate alone with his conflicted feelings. Leaving him to wait and wonder if history might be about to repeat.

CHAPTER SIXTEEN

THE GEORGIAN BUILDING housing Greer's ground-floor flat boasted a small communal garden at the rear that was available to the flat owners for private hire. When Lily returned home from France Saturday evening to find most of her friends and loved ones gathered on the patch of lawn, birthday banners and pretty lanterns strung between the trees, she instantly burst into delighted tears of surprise.

She'd worked so hard for her exams, she deserved this celebration. But with results day looming, Greer only had a few more weeks of having her daughter home before she left for University.

'A private toast to our gorgeous girl,' Greer said, topping up Lily's and Mark's flutes with bubbles and trying to hide her nerves. 'Happy eighteenth birthday. To adulthood and the next phase of your life.'

Lily laughed and Mark added, 'Cheers,' as they clinked glasses, taking a sip.

Mark glanced down at his phone. 'Oh, Cara is here. I'll just go let her in.'

Greer watched him step inside the flat and disappear, her stomach tight with anticipation. She'd slept longer than she'd planned after her busy night and had awoken to several missed calls from the caterers. What with last-minute preparations for the party and the arrival of some horribly early guests, there'd been no time to call Nate, who hadn't yet arrived. Not that she knew what to say. She'd hurt him last night and hoped to find a private moment to apologise. But they both needed to remember that the evening was about Lily.

'So, tell me all about France,' Greer said to her daughter, who looked sun-kissed and happy, her eyes bright with excitement.

At least with Nate a no-show so far, Greer could relax and not have to act *normal* in front of her daughter, Lily's friends and her ex.

'The gîte was stunning, with beautiful views of the vineyards and olive groves and lavender farms,' Lily said. 'I spent so much time in the pool, and Dad hired a car so we could explore all the quaint villages, the beaches and coastal towns.'

'Sounds like you had a magical time. I'm so glad.' Greer gulped some champagne, a part of her sad that once upon a time they'd have taken holidays like that as a family.

But after four years alone, after embracing a fling with Nate, she finally felt strong and resilient. Even if she never fell in love again, she would be okay. She could go to Provence alone—drink wine, sit in cafés, walk on the sand and through fields of lavender.

Just then, as one of Lily's friends joined them, throwing her arms around Lily, Greer looked up to see Mark reappearing from the flat, stepping out into the sunshine with a smiling Cara in tow. And behind them was Nate.

Greer froze, her heart in her throat as her past and present collided. As she'd expected, Nate looked so handsome in chinos, a T-shirt and dark sunglasses, his hair sexily ruffled and his jaw sporting a day's worth of sexy stubble. Longing built like pressure in Greer's chest as she fought the urge to go to him and kiss him as if last night hadn't happened. As if they were alone in the garden. Wouldn't Provence be a little more magical with Nate by her side, the wine a little sweeter, the coffee richer, the walk on the sand more uplifting with her hand in his?

But could they truly have a future? Greer had no desire to go back to being the suspicious and jealous one in a partnership and there would always be younger women who fancied Nate. She was forty-three. She didn't have the luxury of time to make another big mistake. And would Nate even want a future with her? The fact that he couldn't seem to forgive himself left Greer to think that he, too, wasn't quite ready for more than a fling. Could she allow herself to develop feelings for someone when the odds were so steeply stacked against them as a couple? She didn't want to end up making a fool of herself, becoming a cliché when it inevitably came to an end because neither of them was quite ready to make it last.

As Mark and Cara paused to speak to Mark's younger sister and her husband, Greer's stare met Nate's. Greer inhaled sharply as a slam of desire struck. And something else, that familiar bitter taste of fear. Could she possibly already have deep feelings for Nate? He'd declared he might have them for her, but was she ready to put her emotional well-being on the line again so soon? For a man who might not be sure, who might be scared to allow himself to be happy because of his past and his unresolved grief?

As if they were the only two people in the garden, Nate sent her a hesitant smile, his eyes lighting up as he headed her way. Greer overheated, her heart fluttering with a mix of excitement and panic. This, inviting him to Lily's party, had been a mistake. What had she been thinking? How would she pretend they were just friends and colleagues in front of all these people, many of whom knew her better than anyone? When all she wanted to do was kiss him and try to explain her conflicted feelings to them both. When if he stepped too close, she'd crave his touch, want to sneak him away from the party and forget everything apart from the way he made her feel when they were together.

'Hi,' she said, her pulse so fast her head spun. He stepped close, as if he might swoop in to kiss her cheek in greeting, and Greer stepped back. 'Can I get you a drink?'

Her voice sounded off. High-pitched. Guilty. As if she was trying way too hard to be casual.

'Sure,' he said, his smile fading. 'A beer would be great.'

She couldn't make out his expression behind the sunglasses but his posture stiffened slightly, telling her she'd hurt him again with her withdrawal. Of course she had. She was acting as if they were strangers, because suddenly this all felt too serious. Too real. Too terrifying.

Greer turned to the drinks table and selected a can of pale ale, Nate's favourite, pouring it into a tall glass. Her hands trembled. A huge part of her wished they were still in their bubble, wished she could send everyone else home and spend this beautiful summer's evening in bed with him until they laughed together again, until her feelings became clear, and matched by Nate's. But now that there was a sliver of hurt and mistrust between them, now that Lily was home, that was no longer an option. Greer needed time. Time to figure out how she really felt about Nate. Time to know if she wanted a real relationship with him. Time to talk to Lily and the other people she loved to let them know she might be ready to move on.

Wearing a strained smile, Nate took the beer she held out to him. 'You didn't call me.'

'I know…' Greer winced at the justified accusation, her stomach knotted by what she should do and say. 'I'm sorry. I slept in then had last-minute party things to sort out. I figured we might get a chance to talk tonight.'

He watched her carefully, taking a sip of beer as he kept his emotions hidden. 'I met your ex and his fiancée on the doorstep,' he said, glancing casually around the garden so to the unobservant their conversation might appear friendly. But the distance between them had never been greater. Greer felt the tension rolling off him. Felt the same in herself. Torn. Wanting him. Feeling guilty that she'd hurt him. Certain that if she wasn't careful, her secret fling would be exposed to everyone there for Lily.

'What did you tell them?' she asked with a nervous croak, certain that Mark would likely press Nate on who'd invited him because Nate was too old to be a friend of Lily's.

'I told them we just worked together.' He met her stare, his expression blank. 'That you'd invited some of the staff from the emergency department.' His expression hardened and Greer almost reached out to touch his arm. 'Isn't that what you wanted?'

'Yes. Thank you.' She nodded, feeling remorseful and confused. She'd done this. Created the mess she now found herself in. She'd begun this relationship in spite of her reservations. She'd allowed her trust issues to resurface. She'd hurt Nate last night and again today by foolishly inviting him there.

Nate sighed and held up a small gift bag, changing the subject. 'I brought this for Lily.'

Greer smiled as if her face were carved from wood, her heart pounding with both longing and unease at his gesture. 'That's so thoughtful… She's here.'

They joined the small group of young women, who were excitedly talking about their results and which place at uni they were going to select.

'Lily,' Greer said, her chest tight and heart racing, 'you remember Nate Hunter, my colleague in the emergency department.' The words felt awkward as she articulated them but she couldn't seem to make this situation she'd created any better. She just had to hold it together and see it through. Pretend. For Lily.

Lily smiled, despite being so obviously a little taken aback that Nate had been invited. She was probably wondering who this man was, and Greer knew there would be questions later. She'd have to explain herself and hope that Lily wasn't too appalled that her mother had been dating a younger man. That this didn't ruin their last few weeks of them living together.

'Happy Birthday,' Nate said, breezing over the moment. 'I got you a small gift.'

'Thank you,' Lily said with a smile, glancing questioningly at Greer before peering into the bag. She pulled out two items. The first was a small, framed star certificate depicting a celestial constellation with Lily's name at the centre.

'You named a star after me?' Lily said, her eyes wide with delight and surprise as she grinned at Nate.

Nate shrugged. 'Every lover of the universe needs their own star.'

Greer's pulse jerked. A week ago she'd have loved Nate's thoughtfulness, but now she couldn't help but feel that his gift was also an obvious declaration that they were more than friends. Would everyone at the party notice when she'd asked him to keep tonight about Lily and not them?

When Lily opened the second item, a small velvet box, Greer saw a delicate gold chain with an unusual hexagonal pendant and a wave of nausea struck even as she tried to smile for her daughter's sake.

'It's part of a meteorite,' Nate said. 'There's some information in the bag about its structure and where it was found.'

'It's beautiful. Thank you,' Lily said, handing the box to Greer so she could remove the necklace and fasten it around Lily's neck.

'I'm going to show Dad,' she said, rushing off, her friends in tow.

Greer glanced at her feet, a metallic taste in her mouth. 'That was… Thank you.' Greer looked up to see the flicker of hurt in his stare now that he'd pushed his sunglasses up onto his head. 'Of course, it puts me in a tricky position. I hadn't planned on telling Lily about us tonight but she's too smart not to connect the dots.' She winced and dropped her gaze from his, too strung out to think beyond the implications for her and Lily.

'I'm sorry,' he said stiffly. 'I didn't think it would be an issue, given you'd invited me to her birthday party. I didn't want to turn up empty-handed and I see other people also brought gifts.' He tilted his head towards the table near the flat where people had deposited gifts and cards.

Miserable, she nodded and glanced at the other guests to see who might be watching their conversation. 'Maybe this wasn't my finest idea…' she muttered. 'I don't think I'm ready to answer questions about us.' She met his stare, her throat tight. 'I didn't want to hurt you. I guess, on some level, I thought that if Mark was bringing Cara, I could bring a plus one too.'

Nate nodded, his disappointed stare not quite

meeting hers. 'I wondered if you'd told Lily you were dating. Now I see that you haven't.'

Greer swallowed the lump in her throat. 'Nate…' She flushed, unable to find the right words to make this better. 'I did plan to tell her. I just haven't had the right moment yet.'

'I understand.' His voice was flat.

Behind Nate, Lily summoned Greer over, and she reached for the lifeline. 'Listen, I can't do this right now. Lily wants me. Mingle for a while, and I'll be back as soon as I can. We will talk. I promise.'

But as her fears built—fear of hurting or disappointing Lily, fear of making another mistake with Nate and hurting him too if the relationship became any more serious, fear that she should have known better than to think she was ready for another relationship so soon—Greer's stomach sank. Maybe she was better off alone after all.

An hour later, after too much small talk where he'd had to repeat the lie Greer had told her friends and family, that they were just work colleagues, Nate numbly stepped inside the cool shade of the flat out of the evening sun. He'd arrived at the party hoping to find a quiet moment with Greer to declare his feelings, face to face. All of his feelings. But the moment their eyes had met across the lawn, he'd seen the growing divide between them so clearly.

Where he was certain he wanted more than a fling, that he wanted a real relationship, Greer was clearly miles behind. Not that they'd had more than that initial moment to themselves this evening. It was almost as if she was avoiding him purposely.

Leaving his unfinished glass of beer on the kitchen counter, he moved through the flat towards the bathroom and Greer's bedroom beyond, catching sight of her reapplying her lip gloss in the mirror above the chest of drawers to the side of her bed.

'I might head off,' he said, when she spotted him and started as if guilty as sin. 'Thanks for inviting me. I hope Lily enjoys the rest of her party.'

His stomach sank. He understood her obligations. He even understood her fears. But feeling the way he did about her, watching her smile and laugh and not being able to be with her, he couldn't stay and pretend for a second longer.

'Really?' Greer frowned, her eyes darting down the hallway behind him. 'Well, thanks for coming.' Obviously satisfied that there was no one watching, she stepped closer and touched his arm. 'And thank you for your thoughtful gifts. Lily loves them. I'm sorry that we haven't had much chance to talk.'

Nate shrugged, her touch both food for a starving man and a reminder that when it came to their connection, to their willingness to be emotionally vulnerable, to their desires for a real relationship, they were clearly poles apart. For Greer, the 'work colleagues' explanation wasn't a lie. They *were* just colleagues. Colleagues with benefits. Whereas Nate had started to develop feelings for her, convincing himself that she might return those feelings. That she respected him as much as he respected her. Trusted him. But if he was honest, he'd seen the truth in her eyes the day before, after he'd confessed his secret.

Sensing his discomfort, Greer dropped her hand. 'Maybe we can find time to talk tomorrow night at the hospital. We're on the night shift together.'

She offered this as consolation when Nate saw it all too clearly. He might have finally confided his greatest mistake, opened himself up to her judgement because he trusted Greer, wanted to keep dating her and see where this could go, but for Greer, he was just her shameful secret. Someone else she couldn't fully trust.

'Maybe…'

'Or…' she went on, looking uncomfortable, 'maybe we should pause things for a while. Pick up again once Lily has left for Manchester.' She couldn't quite meet his stare and for Nate this was the final blow.

Aching for the return of her touch, but determined to protect himself, Nate pulled back his shoulders. 'Actually, Greer, I'm not sure this is working for me any longer,' he said, recalling her horrified expression when he'd told her about Maggie, her jealousy and withdrawal. Her embarrassment tonight. He'd laid himself bare to her, and Greer was busy retreating. She'd enjoyed the sex but clearly wasn't ready to take this relationship or him seriously.

'Okay…' She frowned, glancing behind him once more to make sure they were still alone. 'I mean, we agreed it would be temporary so… that's fine.'

'Fine?' Nate snorted out a bitter laugh. 'Just like that, huh? You give up on us so easily. But then I think you gave up before tonight. As if I meant nothing to you. As if everything we've shared meant even less.'

She raised her chin defensively. 'You're the one ending it. I told you I needed time. Some space.'

'Because I have feelings for you, Greer.' Nate winced. She looked confused and hurt but most of all guilty. Because he'd been right in his suspicions. 'And I know you can't return those feelings. You don't even trust me. If you did you wouldn't be jealous over nothing. You wouldn't be so ashamed of us. You'd be ready to tell your daughter, your ex, our colleagues about us.'

'That's not true… I do care about you… I just… This isn't the time for this. I have to think about Lily right now. I have a flat full of guests and only a few weeks before she leaves home. I thought you understood.'

Nate nodded in defeat. 'I do understand. I know she's your biggest priority. Just like I know I'm not even a consideration or an afterthought. I'm just a secret you're ashamed of.'

'I'm not ashamed of you… I—'

'Then you're scared,' he said, needing to leave before his humiliation crushed him. 'You think that if you admit our relationship is more meaningful than a fling I'm going to hurt you. When you said you trusted me. But your repeated jealousy proves you don't trust me one little bit.'

'I'm trying my best.' She swallowed and Nate realised he'd struck a nerve. 'But you did keep a secret from me.'

Nate sighed heavily in defeat, her words like a slap. 'Only because I was ashamed of my actions, because it's my biggest regret. I was scared to let you down, the way I let my beloved brother and myself down. Scared to see your judgement, to lose you because you can't handle my relationship with Maggie and Callum. I tore myself open for you, Greer.'

She shook her head, her cheeks red. 'I didn't mean to judge. But part of me couldn't help but think if there's nothing to tell between you and Maggie, why hide it, especially when I've confided in you about my trust issues? I've opened up too, Nate.'

Nate closed his eyes, his devastation building. He was losing her, every word of this conversation he should never have begun pushing her further away. Or maybe he'd never truly had Greer in the first place.

When he looked at her once more, saw her fear and determination, he knew it was over. 'Until today, I was willing to wait for you, Greer. To take this relationship at your pace, because I understood those trust issues. Just like I understood your obligations to your family. But today I saw that I was kidding myself that you could care about me. I don't think you were ever going to tell Lily about us. I don't think you ever had any intention of giving this relationship a real chance.'

'That's not true… I just… This is all new to me. I panicked…'

Nate nodded, hardening his resolve. 'You say you don't want to let Lily down, but you're letting yourself down instead. You're just scared to put yourself first. You said that *I'm* scared to allow myself to be happy because of Dylan, and you're right. But you're scared, too, Greer. Scared to be fully vulnerable with me or any other man. Scared to embrace what we have and make it work.'

'I…' She reached out to touch him again then let her arm fall to her side, deflated.

Nate stepped back. 'Your trust issues have already played a part in the demise of one relationship. I don't want to be the second casualty.' Nate winced because his impulsive mistake with Maggie had now also cost *him* two relationships. 'I don't want to fall in love with you only to lose you, too. Fall in love with you and then feel as if I should choose between you and Dylan's family.'

Greer gasped. 'I would never ask you to choose me over your family. Now who's too scared to trust?'

Just then, the approach of heels tapping on the hardwood floor made Nate turn in time to see one of the guests, most likely a friend of Lily's, round the corner from the living room and head into the bathroom.

'I'll let you get back to the party,' Nate said with a guilty wince. 'Apologies for my timing. I shouldn't have come today. I thought you inviting me, insisting yesterday that you still wanted me here, was a step in the right direction for us, but now I see I was at most just your plus one.'

'Nate, I…'

'Don't worry about it, Greer. There's no point either of us pursuing something that just isn't going to work. I'm sure you'd agree.'

'I'm sorry,' she whispered.

'Me too,' he said, aching for her even as he stepped further away. 'Bye, Greer.'

Forcing himself to leave before the feelings he'd had for her could cut any deeper, he turned and let himself out of the flat.

CHAPTER SEVENTEEN

GREER RINSED THE last of the champagne flutes and placed it upside down on the drainer, her head filled with images of Nate. His hurt and disappointment and devastation. His words, accusations, the raw honesty of his feelings.

Shame washed over her in hot waves, stealing her breath and making her cringe inwardly until she braced her hands on the edge of the sink, her shoulders hunched and her head hung. After he'd left, after she'd emerged from under the weight of what she'd said and how she'd behaved, she'd shut herself in her bedroom and tried to call him to apologise again. When he hadn't answered she'd sent a frantic message: I'm sorry that I hurt you. That wasn't my intention.

She wanted him to see her message even though she needed to spend time with Lily tonight and time figuring out what she should do next. Telling herself that the dark empty place inside her was only a temporary feeling and a result of having hurt Nate, Greer dragged in some deep breaths and slapped on her brave face.

In the hallway, Lily called goodbye to the last of her friends and shut the front door. Greer hurriedly wiped her hands on a kitchen towel and squared her shoulders, pretending, when Lily found her a moment later, that everything was normal.

'Did you enjoy the party?' Greer asked as Lily walked over and held Greer in a tight hug.

'It was amazing. Thanks, Mum. I had no idea you were planning that. Dad said you did everything. That his only contribution was get me there on time.'

'You're welcome.' Greer inhaled a shaky breath, her doubts that she'd done the right thing in breaking it off with Nate building. 'It wasn't difficult to gather people who wanted to help you celebrate becoming an adult. You have a great group of friends.'

Lily's life, her future, were rich and joyful and full of adventure. But what about Greer? She'd acted cowardly today. That was no kind of way for a role model to behave. She'd allowed her fear of being hurt again to stop her from seeing what was right in front of her face. What had been there for days, maybe even weeks. She had feelings for Nate. Huge feelings.

Lily collapsed onto the sofa with a tired sigh and a content smile. 'An adult… That sounds serious. I've asked work for some extra shifts so I can earn as much money as possible in the next few weeks.'

'Good idea…' Greer said distractedly.

Lily nodded and twisted to rest her folded arms on the back of the sofa and her chin on top. 'Are you okay, Mum? Was it hard for you having Dad and Cara here together? I was a bit concerned.'

'It was fine.' Greer gingerly took a seat beside her daughter, feeling as if one wrong move might shatter her into jagged shards. 'If she's going to be your stepmother, I want to get to know Cara better, because I only really care about you and your happiness.'

Lily winced. 'I don't think I'll ever call her my stepmother, given I'm an adult, but I'm glad you feel that way. Will you…come to the bridesmaid-dress fitting with me Tuesday?'

'Of course. If it's okay with Cara.' Greer nodded bravely, knowing Mark and Cara's wedding would be a trial. Not because she was jealous of Cara, but because, having hurt Nate and let him walk away, she'd sabotaged her own chance at a relationship that had made *her* happy.

Because that was what Nate had brought to her life: optimism, laughter, joy.

'Listen, darling,' she said, 'we need to talk.'

'Okay.'

'About Nate and me,' Greer began. 'For a long time after Dad and I split I wasn't feeling brave enough to think about moving on. But, well, the truth is, he's been more than a friend and colleague these past few weeks. That's why I invited him today. We've been seeing each other. Dating, I guess. Just casually.'

She broke off, a wave of grief hitting her square in the chest. And now it was over. And it was Greer's fault. Nate was right. She'd clung to her mistrust, her fear of being hurt again, and all it had brought her was this vile sense of failure and shame and an understanding that she'd ruined the one thing she'd wanted. The one thing she deserved. A second chance at a serious, committed, emotionally mature relationship.

No game-playing. No miscommunication and obligation. Just passion and connection and being present in the relationship because there was nowhere else she'd rather be.

Lily glanced down, fingering the pendant around her neck. 'I kind of guessed as much, Mum. I love them both, but his gifts were way too generous for someone who feels casually about you. He obviously cares deeply. So are you a couple, then?'

Greer shook her head, fresh pain stealing her breath. 'No, in fact I think it's actually over now.' Which was ironic because clarity had come at a terrible price. Of course Greer had developed deep romantic feelings for Nate. He was the best man she'd ever met. Their relationship, before she'd messed up, had been the most mature one she'd ever been in, despite their age gap. He gave her space to be herself, to rediscover herself. He liked her just the way she was, warts and all. He believed in her and cheered at her triumphs. And she'd hurt him, allowed him to believe she couldn't trust him and didn't care. She'd ruined a special thing because she was scared.

Lily frowned, looking uncomfortable. 'I'm sorry about that. He seemed really nice.'

Greer glanced up, stunned. 'You talked to him?'

'Yeah,' Lily said, 'mainly about university. He went to Manchester. Did you know that? But he also talked about you a lot.'

'He did?' Greer asked, her voice a hoarse whisper, her throat aching.

Lily nodded. 'It was obvious he really likes you. Even Dad noticed. He said something dismissive in front of Cara and me. That's why they left suddenly, because it started an argument between them.'

Greer gaped. Her silly attempts to hide how she felt about Nate had obviously failed. Clearly everyone else saw what she'd failed to see: how she felt about Nate.

'So why did you break up with him?' Lily asked. 'Is it because he's younger than you? Cos that's a bit shallow, Mum.'

Greer shook her head, ashamed that she had

worried too much about that. 'He broke up with me, actually.'

'Oh… I'm sorry.' Lily winced. 'How do you feel about that?'

Greer searched her feelings, allowing them to all spill free for the first time since Nate had walked out. 'I… I don't blame him. I hurt him, for which I'm very ashamed. I've got hang-ups, obviously. It's not easy to make yourself vulnerable again after a divorce. But I no longer want to be that scared woman I've been for the past four years.

'With you about to leave home, it's forced me to re-evaluate my priorities. I feel stronger now, resilient, ready to face new adventures and challenges, just like you. I'll always be here for you, of course, but it's time I started putting myself first a bit more.'

'I agree.' Lily nodded. 'Do you…? Does he…? Is Nate someone you could be serious about? You'd said that if you met someone you'd tell me.'

Tears stung Greer's eyes but she sniffed them away. 'I… I care about him a lot. I thought maybe he might be…' Before she'd clung to her fear, allowed Nate to think their connection was trivial, hadn't put up a fight for him or shown him how much she cared.

'How would that have made you feel?' she asked, eager for Lily's honest opinion.

'It's not about me, Mum, but I appreciate you

asking.' Her expression became determined and Greer realised that Nate had been right about that, too. She had raised an exceptional young woman. 'I want you to be happy. I'm proud of you for working on yourself and embracing a scary change. You're amazing and I know that when you do find another serious relationship, it will be the right one for you. Because that's all that really matters in relationships, isn't it?'

'Yes, it is.' Greer nodded bravely, blinking away her tears. 'I'm proud of the woman you are, too.'

Lily smiled. 'It's how you taught me to be.'

Greer chuckled. 'Yes, I did, didn't I?'

'So what arc you going to do?' Lily carefully asked, as if she understood the implications Greer was only now waking up to. That Nate might not give her a second chance.

'I'm not sure,' Greer said, her mind racing. 'But whatever happens, I will be fine. I'm strong, like you. I'm excited to rediscover myself now that my daughter will soon be flying the nest. I might want a relationship, but I'm also okay being alone, which sounds lonely but is actually an important life skill. We all have to love ourselves first. And whether I'm alone, or in a relationship, I'll always be your mum. I'll always be here for you and be there to cheer you along.'

'I know that.' Lily nodded, tears building on her eyelashes. 'Love you, Mum.'

Greer smiled, feeling as if she'd reached an important parenting milestone. She was ready to let Lily go. But was she ready to lose Nate without a fight?

By seven the next morning, after a sleepless night, tossing and turning through the lonely hours of darkness, where he'd replayed every word of his argument with Greer, Nate couldn't stand another hour of his own company. Donning his running shoes, he jogged all the way to Callum and Maggie's place five miles away. He needed to see friendly faces. Needed to hear Callum's laughter so he could get out of his own head and hopefully make sense of the way he was feeling: as if he'd been hit by a bus. A feeling that reminded him of grief. But obviously, by grieving for Greer, he was grieving a relationship he'd never actually had apart from in his own imagination.

Arriving at Maggie's place exhausted, his lungs burning because he'd pushed himself so hard as if he could outrun his feelings of loss and devastation, he knocked on the front door.

The curtains twitched and Maggie's haggard face appeared at the living room window. 'Use your key,' she called through the glass. 'I've got a horrible cold.'

Nate used his key to unlock Maggie's front door and stepped into the hallway.

'Stay away from me,' she moaned from the living room, her voice thick and nasal-sounding. 'I'm horribly germ-ridden. I don't want you to catch it.'

Nate poked his head into the room to see Maggie flaked out on the sofa, her eyes and nose red and used tissues scattered over the floor. 'Where's Callum? Is he okay?'

'He's fine,' she said, waving her hand. 'My dad has taken him to the park to burn off some energy. That kid bounces back from a cold after one day whereas I'm poleaxed for a week.'

Nate's stomach sank. Looked as if he'd be alone with himself after all.

'Can I get you anything while I'm here?' he asked, keeping his distance. 'I was out for a run and thought I'd pop in to see my favourite nephew.'

'I'm out of tissues,' she said, sniffling. 'There's a new box in the cupboard under the stairs. You can toss them to me so you don't have to come too close.'

Nate located the box and did as she asked, hesitating in the doorway as if he had no idea where to go next.

'What's wrong?' Maggie asked, blowing her nose and then pushing herself up on her elbows.

'Nothing,' Nate automatically replied. 'I—' He couldn't even find the words to describe the sickening emptiness he was feeling.

'Oh no, Nate,' Maggie said. 'It's over, isn't it? You and your work colleague. The "nice lady with the big smile", as Callum calls her.'

Nate shrugged, weariness slumping his shoulders. 'Yeah… I think it is.'

'Really? Why?' Maggie sat all the way up now, the balled-up tissue sliding from her lap onto the floor to join the others. 'I thought you really liked her.' She looked appalled, personally affronted, as if she was invested in Nate's happiness, counting on the relationship to restore her faith in romance after her own loss.

'I did. Do. But… Well, it's just not going to work out.' And maybe it was for the best. Relationships took time and effort. Better to know now that Greer wasn't interested and couldn't trust him before his feelings got any deeper. Although he'd never felt this crushed after a break-up before.

'I'm so sorry to hear that,' Maggie said softly, blinking away tears.

'Hey, it's okay,' he said, feeling sick because his heartache had obviously reminded Maggie of her own over Dylan. 'I'm going to be fine, just like I know you are too, one day. When you're ready. There's no one like Dylan, but nor is he the only awesome man out there. We're both going to move on eventually and find love again and—'

Nate stopped abruptly, nausea burning the back of his throat as realisation struck. They weren't simply feelings he had for Greer. He wasn't simply at risk of falling in love with her or headed in that direction. He *was* in love with her. Utterly and completely. That explained why he currently felt like half a man. Why he couldn't stand his own company. Why, if he prodded his devastation too closely, he knew he'd find fear that he might not survive.

Realising what he'd done and, more importantly, what he hadn't done, Nate gripped the back of his neck and stared blindly at the wall, his vision tunnelling. Greer was right; he was scared to allow himself to be happy. Because Dylan wasn't around to feel the same. Because Nate loved Dylan and it hadn't been enough to save him. Not only was he scared it might happen again, that he'd lose Greer and be broken once more, he was also scared to rip himself completely open and tell her exactly how he felt and what he wanted. Otherwise he'd have realised his feelings sooner and confessed them last night.

Nate swore under his breath, his mind reliving their break-up. He'd been so scared to chase happiness he'd thought he didn't deserve that, when she'd wobbled over her jealous impulses, he'd convinced himself he couldn't give Greer the time she might need to break the news of their relationship to Lily and ended the thing he wanted the most. Before he could get hurt again.

'It's not too late to tell her,' Maggie said, tears

spilling freely from the corners of her eyes as, somehow, she managed to understand the realisations Nate had just come to before him.

He frowned in confusion, but of course Maggie understood his feelings better than he had. She was still deeply in love with Dylan. She knew all about loss and regret.

But Maggie and Dylan had known deeply committed love. The kind Nate knew he could no longer live without. The kind he knew himself capable of with Greer, if only he could forgive himself his regrets and tell Greer exactly how he felt and what he wanted.

'I have to go,' Nate said, turning towards the front door. He had to tell Greer. Now. Had to beg her to give him another chance.

'Yes. Go!' Maggie waved him away, calling after him, 'Be brave. Tell her everything. Chances are rare and so is love.'

Too desperate to reply, Nate let himself out of the house and raced towards the Tube station. Then, deciding it was better to keep on the move, that he had no patience to wait for the train, he bypassed the station and carried on running the two miles to Greer's flat, praying that she'd be home when he got there. That she'd talk to him. Give him an opportunity to say everything he'd been too scared to say the night before. He hoped it wasn't too late.

Twenty minutes later as he turned into Greer's

street, his heart pounding with fear and sweat stinging his eyes, Nate spotted Greer at her front door.

Dressed in exercise clothes and wearing trainers, headphones around her neck, she was obviously on her way to the gym or going for a walk. Just going about her day as if unaffected by the loss and devastation Nate felt now that their relationship was over.

He watched in horror as Greer withdrew her key from the lock and walked down the path towards the pavement. Nate sprinted the last few metres to get to her before he missed his chance. Maybe it was already too late. Maybe she'd moved on. Maybe he might pour out all of his heart and she still wouldn't want him. Either way, he owed it to himself, to the transformative relationship they'd had and to Greer, to find out.

CHAPTER EIGHTEEN

PAUSING ON THE path from her front door, Greer tried to breathe through the pain and panic tightening her chest as her key dug into her palm inside her clenched fist. She'd dressed for a walk, hoping a brisk round of the park in the sun might help her put everything into perspective, help her escape her sickening thoughts and fears and brutal recriminations. But it was no use. No amount of exercise or reasoning would banish how she felt—bereft, helpless, untethered. The only way to stop the pain was to see Nate and apologise. To ask him to give her a second chance. Not tonight when they'd be working the night shift together. But now.

Resolved to head for the Tube instead of the park, she paused to open the gate, looked up and sucked in a harsh breath. 'Nate… What are you doing here?'

He stood on the street, his hair and T-shirt damp with sweat and his chest heaving as if he'd run the London Marathon.

'I…need to talk to you,' he said, catching his breath. Reaching for her hand as if she might flee.

Greer nodded frantically as hope surged. 'Come inside. Lily is at work. I… I was just going for a walk to clear my head but changed my mind and decided to go to your place. I need to apologise to you, Nate.' Desperate to get him inside so she could say all the things she wanted, Greer shoved her key back into the lock.

'Wait,' he said, gripping her shoulders and spinning her to face him. 'I need to tell you this. Now. It's important.'

Greer nodded, her stomach twisted with fear. He was really there. Surely that meant she had a chance.

'I'm in love with you, Greer,' he said, exhaling a ragged sigh of relief. 'That's what I should have told you last night. But I freaked out and got scared and sabotaged us instead.'

Greer blinked in disbelief, her eyes stinging with unshed tears. Could he mean it? Could she finally be honest with him and herself and earn a second chance?

'You were right about me,' he went on in a rush. 'I have been scared to allow myself to be happy. Scared to forget Dylan. I… I felt responsible for him as I always had. I let my little brother down, twice, and I don't think I'll ever stop grieving for him. But I *do* forgive myself. I can't let what happened, the mistake I made, hold me back any longer. Not when it's holding me back from you. Dylan wouldn't want that and I don't want it either. I want *you.* I don't want us to be over. I'll wait for as long as it takes for you.'

'Nate…' she choked out, her throat aching.

'I know.' He shook his head as if shaking out the memories of the hurt. 'I said terrible things last night that I regret.' He pulled her closer. 'Of course, I'm willing to wait for you to feel comfortable with us. You have every right to tell Lily about us in your own time. My gifts were too much. Just please…give me another chance to be with you. I'm in love with you. I'm crazy about you as you deserve and I will be for the rest of my life if you'll let me.'

Greer reached up and cupped his face between her palms. 'Nate—' Her voice broke. 'I think I love you too,' she blurted, feeling foolish that she hadn't realised the depth of her feelings sooner. Because of course she loved him. Desperately. He was everything she wanted and deserved. And she was no longer afraid of being vulnerable with him.

'You do?'

Greer nodded. 'And I know I deserve you. I was stuck when I met you. Afraid to focus on myself because starting over emotionally felt so… enormous. But you wanting me, pursuing me, it jolted me out of my inertia. You are a wonderful man. In every way.'

He frowned as if he didn't believe her, and she took his hands in hers, smiling a watery smile. 'You were right about me, too. I am scared. The power of this, of us, the connection we've had from the start…it terrified me. I convinced myself that I was okay alone. That I had peace of mind and needed to focus on raising my daughter, but I was hiding behind that. I needed more. I needed *you.* This is the most mature and mutually respectful relationship I've ever had. Real grown-up stuff. I didn't know how I would ever be this vulnerable with someone else after my divorce, but you made it easy. I don't want to be scared any longer. I want to put my needs and passions first. I want to embrace my strengths and love again with every part of my heart. I want you, too, Nate.'

A fiercely possessive expression came over his face as he cupped her cheeks. 'I love you so much.' Then his mouth covered hers, lips parting, breaths sighing, tongues duelling as they clung to each other in the street with the morning sun streaming through the filter of the plane trees lining the pavement.

'Come inside,' she said when they came up for air. With her hand in his, she quickly unlocked the outer door and the flat door and pulled him inside, her heart soaring with joy.

'I told Lily about us after the party last night,' she said, everything she wanted him to know rushing out. 'I'm so sorry for my jealousy or if I made you feel you weren't a priority or that I was ashamed of you. You were right. I allowed my trust issues from the past to blur everything I was feeling for you. But after you left, after I thought it was over, those feelings became so obvious.'

He shook his head, reaching for her once more. 'I gave up on us, too. Some part of me obviously realised I was falling in love with you. I got scared to lose you. Scared that I'd tell you about Maggie and lose you or that I'd love you so hard, I'd lose you another way. But I promise you I won't ever give up on us again, Greer,' he added, kissing her lips, her cheeks, her eyelids. 'I won't let you down or hurt you. Ever. I want you exactly as you are—strong and compassionate and smart and sure of yourself and sexy and funny.'

'I know you won't,' she said, holding him tight. 'I trust you, Nate.' Flinging her arms around his neck, she tugged his mouth down to hers. She slid her fingers through his hair and deepened her kiss, smiling when he crushed her body to his.

'We're going to have such amazing adventures,' she said when he released her.

'And amazing sex,' he said, filling his hands with the cheeks of her backside. 'We're going to have lots of sex.'

'Definitely,' she agreed, laughing when he slid his lips down the side of her neck.

'What time is Lily home?' he asked, his hand slipping under her top to caress her breast.

'Four,' she said, mentally calculating how many hours they had between now and then.

'Could you put your hands on one of those stashed condoms?'

'Yes. On more than one if you're up to it.'

'Hold on,' he said, hoisting her from the floor so she wrapped her thighs around his waist and held on as he carried her to the bedroom. 'I need a shower,' he said and he detoured to the en suite bathroom where they quickly discarded their clothes and, laughing, both stepped under the spray.

'I love you,' Greer said, rubbing shower gel over his chest, spreading the scented suds everywhere her hands glided as Nate groaned and clutched her close, his lips roaming her neck and face. 'I'm ready to bring our relationship into the daylight. To embrace it and love every minute of being with you.'

Nate pressed her slippery body to his hard one, his arms steely bands around her. 'Do you believe that I'm all for you? That I'm a one-woman man? That you are everything I could possibly want? Almost too hot for me to handle?'

She smiled, laughed, pressed her lips to his as the water cascaded over them, washing away the suds. 'Yes. I know you. I know your strength and compassion. I know your heart and your passion. I know I'm safe with you and that this is the place I want to be.'

She wrapped her arms around his shoulders and kissed him as he turned off the shower. After the briefest of rub-downs with a towel, they hurried to Greer's bed. Every touch and caress felt like a promise. Every kiss reaffirmed their connection. Every groan and moan and whisper brought them impossibly closer so when, finally, hearts racing and breath panting, Nate pushed inside her, Greer knew that their happiness as a couple was in their hands.

Nate dragged in deep breath after deep breath, the powerful aftershocks of his orgasm tensing every muscle in his body. Turning his head, he buried his nose in Greer's silky hair and sucked in the scent of her skin. With him still buried inside her, it was impossible for them to get closer physically, but still he craved that, as if he were still scared of losing her.

'I love you,' he whispered against her ear as their hearts banged side by side. 'I never want to let you go.'

'I love you, too.' Greer pulled back and smiled with satisfaction, pressing kisses all over his face as the euphoric high lingered.

After a quick trip to the bathroom, Nate returned, sliding into Greer's bed and drawing her back into his arms. 'How did Lily take the news about us?' he asked, his heart rate accelerating once more. 'Is she okay?' He didn't want to ever be a source of conflict between Greer and her daughter, who had such a close bond.

'She took it like the intelligent mature woman she is,' Greer said with a proud smile as she lazily ran her fingers through his hair. 'Said she liked you and just wanted me to be happy. She said she knew I'd only enter into another relationship if it was absolutely right for me, which this one is.'

Nate nodded, his chest tightening. 'So we're in a real relationship, then?' He flashed her a sexy grin, elated.

Greer laughed and nodded, her smile breathtaking. 'You make me happy,' she said, cupping his face. 'You give me a safe space in which to heal and find myself and be strong.'

'And you give me everything I've ever wanted.' He cupped her chin and kissed her softly.

'Are you sure you don't want kids of your own?' she asked when she pulled back, her beautiful stare shining with love but also the last glimmer of fear. 'Because I think I'm too old now. Past that phase of my life.'

'I'm sure.' Nate brought her hand up to his mouth and kissed her fingers. 'I want you, Greer. I want to share my life with you. I want to be a part of yours. I want to travel with you and laugh with you and hold you and be there for you. You are all I'll ever need.'

Greer nodded, a relieved smile on her lips. 'Me too.'

'About Callum,' he said, his voice thick with emotion. 'I hope he'll always be a part of my life.'

'Of course he will. I understand your bond. It's one of the reasons I love you. And I know you're scared to forget Dylan, but how could you when you have Callum as a reminder? When Dylan is a part of you too?' She pressed her hand to his chest over the thump of his heart.

'I love you,' he said roughly, pressing his lips back to hers. Before he could become distracted by her kisses, Nate added, 'I know one day Maggie will be ready to move on. She's still desperately in love with my brother—she cried for him, for their love, when I told her I'd almost lost you. I think she could see I was in love with you before it finally struck me. But one day, there'll likely be another man in Callum's life and that's fine with me.'

'You'll always be his Uncle Nate.'

'I will,' he said, hoping that Dylan could rest knowing that Nate would always be there for his son.

Greer smiled lovingly, sliding her fingers through his hair. 'Maybe we could get Maggie and Callum over for a barbecue before Lily goes to Manchester. It would be good for us all to meet properly.'

'It would,' he agreed, his heart pounding with

another wave of love for this incredible woman. 'If we're all going to be a funny little family of sorts.'

She nodded, her fingertip tracing his cheekbone and the line of his jaw. 'That we are. How would you feel if I resigned from Kensington Hospital?'

He froze, his heart lurching. 'Is that really necessary? I want to work with you.'

'I want to work with you too,' she said. 'But it would solve the tricky issue of me being your boss. Either way, I'm going to inform HR that we're an item.'

Nate's arms tightened around her, his lips grazing hers as if he'd forgotten their taste. 'I love you being my boss. But the other option is that I apply for the next consultant post that arises in our hospital. Then we'd be equals.'

'We're already equals. But if you want that then I'd support you. You're definitely ready.'

'I'd rather we worked at the same hospital if possible. I don't want to miss you.'

'I'd miss you, too.' She smiled and pressed herself against him, bringing their lips back together. 'You just want to lure me back into that on-call room for another quickie, don't you?'

Nate grinned, kissing her once more. 'I mean, you're not wrong. I do. That was seriously hot.' He pushed her hair back from her face and stared deep into her eyes. 'But I'll support whatever decision you make, Greer.'

'Whatever decision *we* make,' she whispered, her breath mingling with his.

Nate nodded. 'As long as you're happy. I want you to be happy and fulfilled and secure.'

'And with you, I am all of those things.'

Nate held her closer, kissed her deeply. His love for her finally free. And because he loved her, because she was naked in his arms, her legs entwined with his, his body responded, becoming aroused again.

Greer pulled back from the heated kiss and gasped in mock delight. 'Again so soon?' she asked teasingly, parting her thighs when her rolled on top of her, her smiling stare, sexy and eager, locked to his. 'Oh, the marvellous benefits of dating a younger man.'

She laughed joyously and Nate kissed her again and again, their playfulness turning into the serious business of loving each other once more.

EPILOGUE

One year later...

GREER HAD DONE her research, discovering that the best time to visit Provence, but also to avoid the crowds, was early July, just before the school year ended. Not that term dates were a concern for Greer any longer. Lily had passed her A levels and breezed through the first year of her degree, making friends, learning new things, even falling in love with a second-year fellow astrophysics student.

'It's utterly breathtaking here,' she said, squeezing Nate's hand as they walked the path between the rows of lavender plants, the warm air sweet with their fragrance and the gentle hum of visiting honeybees.

They'd spent the day exploring Roussillon village, Provence's ochre jewel perched high on a ridge, walking the charming cobbled streets, pausing to enjoy galleries and cafés and take endless photos together, ending the day with a trip to one of the many lavender farms in the valley below.

'There's a table under the trees,' Nate said, plucking a lavender bloom, crushing the flower between his fingers to release the aroma, inhaling the scent before passing it to Greer. 'Let's sit for a while and enjoy the sunset.'

Greer sighed contentedly as they headed for the small copse of trees under which a single table sat with an on-brand purple shade umbrella.

'There's champagne,' she said as they stepped closer, spinning to face a smug-looking Nate. 'Did you organise this?'

'Yes,' he said. 'It seemed like the perfect end to a wonderful day.'

Greer sighed as Nate removed the bottle from a sweating ice bucket and popped the cork, pouring two glasses. He passed her one and took his own, their free hands clasped between them as they stood smiling at each other.

'A toast,' he said, holding up his glass. 'To the best year of my life. Waking up next to you, being in a relationship with you, getting to hold your hand as we shared the highs and lows of our work and daily life is a luxury I won't ever take for granted.'

'Me neither,' Greer whispered, her heart pulsing with the love she felt for this incredible man. Every day she felt lucky that they'd given each other a second chance. Every day, she praised herself for being brave enough to realise that what she wanted and needed was Nate.

'I know you said you never wanted to get married again,' he said as he placed his glass down, 'but I want to spend the rest of my life loving you, Greer.'

As Greer watched with surging excitement, he pulled a box from his pocket. 'If it's as your husband, your common-law partner or even your boy toy with benefits, I want you to have this as a sign of my commitment to us. To you.'

Greer placed her flute down before she dropped it as Nate opened the box and pulled out the stunning ring.

'Nate…' she said on a breathless gasp, her stare searching his to see his feelings for her swimming there.

'I asked Lily for her blessing first,' he said, removing the ring from the box and holding it up.

'You did? What did she say?' Greer shouldn't be surprised. Lily and Nate had become good friends this past year. Lily could go to him for sound, mature advice and Nate never missed an opportunity to know Greer's daughter a little better.

Nate smiled his sexy smile, the one she saw every day. The one she would never take for granted or tire of. 'She said she wanted you to be happy. So it's all over to you.' He held the ring a little higher so the diamond glinted in the sun.

'Yes,' Greer said without hesitation, throwing her arms around his neck. 'I will marry you. I want you to be my husband, as long as we can also keep the boy toy with benefits on the table.' She smiled against his lips as they kissed, his joy igniting her own as he held her in his strong arms, their hearts racing side by side.

'Yeah, we can.' His arms tightened around her waist, his smile the sexy one she adored.

Greer pulled back, cupping his face between her palms. 'I love you, Nate. You're the only man for whom I would make an exception. But know that if you put that ring on my finger, then that's it for ever. Just you and me.'

Nate's smile stretched, his eyes sparkling. 'In that case…' He took her left hand and she spread her fingers as Nate slid the ring onto her finger. 'Now you're mine for ever,' he said, picking her up and twirling her around as the scent of sun-baked lavender filled the warm air. 'And I'm yours.'

He loosened his grip and her body slid down his until her feet touched the ground once more and he kissed her passionately.

'Wait,' Greer said, when she came up for air. 'We didn't drink to the toast. Doesn't that mean we might have seven years' bad sex?' She reached for their glasses of champagne and handed one to him, clinking the flutes together for good luck.

One arm around her waist, Nate held her close

and stared deep into her eyes, his wickedly playful. 'With you? Impossible,' he said, brushing her lips with his and groaning sexily.

'In that case,' she said, because she knew there would never be any worries on that score, 'cheers to years of incredible sex. And to us.'

Holding her stare as if he might suggest a quickie under the trees, a divine possibility for which Greer could muster no reluctance, Nate touched his glass to hers once more, sighed as they each took a sip and then kissed her again.

* * * * *